diary of a
REAL PAYNE

CHURCH CAMP CHAOS

Annie Tipton

BARBOUR
PUBLISHING

Published by Barbour Publishing, Inc., P.O. Box 719, Uhrichsville, Ohio 44683, www.barbourbooks.com

Our mission is to publish and distribute inspirational products offering exceptional value and biblical encouragement to the masses.

Member of the
Evangelical Christian
Publishers Association

Printed in the United States of America.
Dickinson Press, Inc., Grand Rapids, MI 49512; February 2014; D10004316

"For I know the plans I have for you," says the LORD. *"They are plans for good and not for disaster, to give you a future and a hope."*

JEREMIAH 29:11

Dear Diary,

Remember when I started writing in you last summer?
Remember the fun we had and the memories we made?
Wasn't it great? Remember how I got lazy and stopped
writing in you after Christmas?

Yeah, that happened. I'm sorry. The good news is, I'm
back now!

Why did I stop writing in you? I blame the longest,
most frigidest and snowiest winter ever in the history
of Wisconsin. I like snow as much as the next
midwestern girl (sledding and snow forts and
snowmen and snowball fights and ice-skating are
the best!), but by the time January rolled around
and the serious cold set in, most of my daydreams had
something to do with turning into a bear just so I could
actually hibernate until spring. How cold was it? I'm talking
temperatures that would freeze the inside of your nose

(also known as the weirdest feeling ever) the
instant you stepped outside.

During a particularly cold week in

February when the temperature was way below zero every day, Dad decided to do a little arctic weather experiment he'd seen on an Internet video. Of course, this got me and my little brother, Isaac, curious, because the last time Dad tried something he saw on the Internet, it ended with Diet Coke and Mentos (you know, those white, round-shaped mints you can get at the grocery store checkout) sprayed all over the side of the minivan. (Mom wasn't too thrilled about that.)

But with no soda or mints in sight, I asked Dad what he was going to do this time, but he just said to watch and wait. So Dad bundled up like he was going on a long trek through the snow-covered streets. Then he filled a pan with water from the sink and put it on the stovetop to heat up. Again we tried to ask him questions, but he just acted like he couldn't hear us through his toboggan hat and scarf wrapped around his face and ears. When the water got to a good boil, Dad picked the pan up by its handle, pushed through the

kitchen door, and stepped out onto the back patio. Mom, Isaac, and I pressed up against the window to watch. Already we could see billowing steam coming off the hot water in the pan. He pointed at the steam and gave a thumbs-up with his gloved hand, and then, without warning, he hurled the boiling water up into the air!

(Side note: I'm just a kid, Diary, but even I know throwing boiling water up in the air would normally be a supremely dumb idea. . .but in subzero temperatures, something almost like magic happened.)

The instant the water hit the freezing air, it burst into an exploding cloud of white snow and ice that fell back to the ground as the wind blew it toward the swing set at the edge of the backyard. In two words, it was *spectacularly magnificent.*

Now it's May, and I think it's safe to say spring has finally arrived in Spooner, Wisconsin. This is the time of year when the entire state steps outside, breathes in a chestful of fresh spring air, and dances a little jig of happiness. Isaac's jig is the goofiest of all. He kicks his legs back behind him and throws his head back. He is convinced that if he tries hard enough, he'll be able to kick himself in the back of the head.

At least the kid has goals, I guess.

There are only three days of school left till summer vacation. (Can you hear the students of Spooner Elementary shouting, "Hallelujah"?) I never thought I'd say this, Diary, but fourth grade hasn't been so bad. Sure, the year started out a little rough when I thought Ms. Picky Pickerington and I wouldn't get along, but after the school spelling bee in the fall when I came in second place, Ms. P started to warm up to me. She even began calling me "EJ" instead of "Emma Jean." Well, she tried.

> Ms. P: [not looking up from the papers she's grading at her desk] EG, would you hand out one of these worksheets to each student, please?
> [Awkward silence in the classroom]
> Ms. P: [looking up at me over the top of her reading glasses] MJ, didn't you hear me?

Please come hand out these worksheets to your classmates.

[I continue to look down at my desk, concentrating on the math problem in front of me. My classmate CoraLee taps me on the shoulder, points toward Ms. P, and smirks at me.]

Me: What? Ms. P? Are you talking to me?

Ms. P: I most certainly am, Eee-Jaaay. If you aren't going to respond to your initials, then perhaps I should go back to calling you by your real name, Emma Jean—

Me: No! I mean, no thank you, Ms. P. I was just making the numbers line up in perfect columns on my multiplication worksheet—just like you like them. I promise to listen more carefully for my name, ma'am.

Ms. P: See that you do, AJ. See that you do.

From then on, I pretty much answered Ms. P anytime I heard the letters E or J come out of her mouth.

CoraLee McCallister is still mostly

terrible. She doesn't know it was me, my family, and our neighbor Mr. Johnson who helped them a few months ago when CoraLee's dad was out of work and they didn't have money for Christmas presents. Let me tell you, Diary, there have been so many times when CoraLee is being not nice to me that I want to blurt out the secret—just so I could see the look of shock and surprise on her face! But the truth is I kind of like knowing something she doesn't know (it makes me feel a good kind of sneaky), and even though CoraLee isn't the nicest person on the planet, I'm honestly glad we helped the McCallisters.

Speaking of CoraLee, she and I both competed in the regional spelling bee in February after we came in first (CoraLee) and second (me) in the Spooner Elementary spelling bee last fall. And guess what. I won!

Okay, that's not entirely true. I went out in the eighth round on the word *accommodate* when I left out an *m*. But I did get further in the competition than CoraLee did! She went out in the fifth round on the word *panicked*, which, if I'm being 100 percent honest, is a pretty tricky word. I'm counting the fact that I outlasted CoraLee as a big win for me!

Isaac started losing baby teeth on his sixth birthday on April 6, so he's looking even weirder than normal with one top tooth and one bottom tooth missing. And now that he knows about the tooth fairy and the cash he can score, he's constantly trying to pull teeth before they're ready to come out—or even a tiny bit loose, for

that matter. I told him he'd better stop or he'll be toothless and all he'll be able to eat is mashed-up bananas. I guess Isaac thought eating mashed-up bananas sounded delicious, because

he immediately started into his best impression of a chimpanzee—scratching his armpits, jumping in place, and screeching, "Ooo! Ooo! Ahh! Ahh!" at me.

Ugh. Little brothers.

My eleventh birthday is in just a couple of weeks, so I'm super excited about that. The party is going to be a mystery dinner theater planned by Mom and my favoritest neighbor, Mrs. Winkle! Nana and Pops are going to be visiting from Ohio over my birthday, too. It's going to be fantastic!

There's so much to look forward to this summer, Diary, but the thing I am absolutely, beyond description, outrageously happy about is that I get to go to a whole week of church camp! Yes! It's what I've been waiting for my whole life! No more day camp (for babies!) or overnight camp (for slightly older babies!) but a whole Monday-to-Saturday week of adventure! My best friend, Macy, is going to go to camp, too. Things couldn't be more perfect!

Camp is in July. Is it too early to start packing?

EJ

Chapter 1

School's Out for Summer

Dear Diary,

Tomorrow is the last day of school! Other than

Christmas and my birthday, the last day of

school is the best day of the year. Outdoor

games in the morning (my class is going to

dominate the tug-of-war this year because we have the

biggest boys in all of the fourth grade!) and a picnic at

the park in the afternoon. The bestest of best days.

Isaac has been so excited for the last day of school

that every morning for a month, the first question

out of his mouth has been, "Is today the last day,

Marmalade?" (Can you believe he still calls Mom by

that silly old nickname?) And every day Mom has

answered, "No, it's not the last day quite yet. But it'll

be here soon." After Isaac asked the same question four

days in a row, Mom decided to make a "Last Day of

School Countdown" chart to put on the refrigerator.

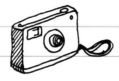
One afternoon she took a bunch of

pictures of us while we made our

best crazy faces. ("Okay, this time I

want you to look so excited that your head is about to explode!"
she said.) She even let my pup, Bert, get
in on the action! What were the pictures
for? We found out the next morning when
Mom unveiled the countdown chart, complete
with little magnets made out of our crazy-face pictures that
we used to cover up each day as we counted down to the last
day. We saved the "so excited our heads are about to explode"
magnets for tomorrow—the last day of school!

EJ

"EJ! Look!" Macy waved her arms excitedly from behind a bench on the Spooner Elementary School playground. "It's like some kind of miracle!"

"What is it, Mace?" EJ crouched down next to her best friend, and peered at the "miracle"—a tiny, crystal-clear butterfly chrysalis hanging from one of the bench's wooden slats. EJ's eyes widened in amazement as she realized she was looking at the black-and-orange wings of a monarch butterfly.

"It's trying to come out," Macy whispered. "Have you ever seen anything so beautiful?"

EJ held her breath as the chrysalis quivered and the bottom split open. A few seconds later, the butterfly began to emerge, sliding out a fraction of an inch while its tiny black legs scrambled furiously to escape its see-through prison.

After about a minute, the entire butterfly was out and clinging to the empty shell of the chrysalis as it unfolded its brand-new wings and took a couple of tentative trial flaps.

"That. Was. Awesome," Macy said. "Think of it, EJ! That little guy just completely changed. A whole new identity!"

"Like a superhero—and it can even fly!" EJ said, grinning. "I bet he's not sorry to say good-bye to his lame caterpillar body."

"What are you two dorks doing back there?" CoraLee perched high on her knees on the bench and sneered down at them.

EJ opened her mouth to tell CoraLee to buzz off, but the almost-always-nice Macy started to speak first.

"We found a butterfly that just came out of its chrysalis—come look, CoraLee!" Macy scooted over to make room for CoraLee. EJ decided she wouldn't budge an inch.

"Gross!" CoraLee scrunched her nose in disgust and cupped

her hands around her mouth, shouting, "MS. PICKERINGTON, EJ IS OVER HERE PLAYING WITH BUGS!"

"CoraLee, what is your *problem?*" EJ jumped to her feet and rounded the bench, coming at CoraLee with gritted teeth and fists at her sides. "We're not hurting anyone or anything!"

CoraLee put her hands on her hips, nose in the air. "Ms. P. thinks proper young ladies shouldn't play with bugs, *Emma Jean.*"

Ms. Pickerington, wearing a sun visor on her head and a whistle around her neck for field day, marched up to the girls in a huff. "CoraLee, what's all the shouting about? It's time for fourth grade to head down to the soccer field for tug-of-war and relay races."

"EJ is playing with bugs." CoraLee used her best tattletale voice and aimed her pointer finger right at EJ's nose, so close that EJ's eyes crossed a little bit.

"Ms. P, ma'am, we aren't playing with bugs." Macy stepped from behind the bench, her hands behind her back. "We were watching a butterfly come out of its chrysalis. See?" Macy revealed her left hand, palm up, where the small butterfly remained for a second before flapping its wings to take off on its first wobbly flight.

"Oh, how lovely." Ms. P's breath caught in her throat as she watched the delicate creature flit toward the monkey bars.

A few moments later, Ms. P snapped out of her trance and turned back to the girls. EJ braced herself for the scolding she was sure was about to come out of her teacher's mouth.

"CoraLee, it would do you well to mind your own business, dear," Ms. P said, pursing her lips. "In other words, I think you should try to be less of a tattletale."

"What? I mean, are you serious?" CoraLee looked shocked. But EJ looked even more shocked, her mouth hanging open, glancing back and forth between her teacher and classmate.

"Quite serious," Ms. P said. "Now, CoraLee, please go to the soccer field with the rest of the fourth graders. We'll be there shortly."

Speechless, CoraLee shot one more spiteful look at EJ before stomping toward the rec field, cross-armed and red-faced.

"You know, EJ, I'm proud of you," Ms. P said.

"Proud of me?" EJ looked confused. "For playing with bugs?"

"No, no." A smile tugged at the corners of Ms. P's mouth. "I'm proud of you, because the Emma Jean Payne I met at the beginning of fourth grade was too busy imagining herself doing a space walk on top of the monkey bars to see the miracles going on around her every day—like the transformation of that butterfly."

"Well, to be honest, Ms. P," EJ said, jabbing her thumb toward Macy. "It wasn't me who found it. It was Macy."

"Then good for you for picking your friends wisely," Ms. P said. "And Macy, thanks for keeping EJ's feet on the ground. I can tell you two balance each other out."

EJ and Macy smiled at each other. Even though Macy was in a different fourth-grade class, she'd heard the stories (mostly from EJ) about how hard it was to stay on Ms. P's good side.

"Okay, girls, let's get down to the soccer field so our class can beat your class in the fourth-grade tug-of-war, Macy," Ms. P said with an uncharacteristic twinkle in her eye.

"You're on, Ms. P!" Macy said.

Twenty minutes later, after Ms. P's class had won the tug-of-war tournament, the fourth graders were preparing to start a three-legged race.

EJ tugged on the rope that tied one of Macy's and EJ's knees together.

"Is it supposed to be this tight?" EJ asked.

"It needs to be snug like that so we can run like we're one person," Macy said, looking around at their competition. "We're lucky we're so close to being the same height." She nodded toward a handful of kids practicing on the sidelines. "CoraLee and Sara are going to have a tough time."

Sara Powers was a girl in EJ's class who had started an impressive growth spurt the summer before fourth grade and now was at least a foot taller than anyone their age—boy or girl. It was pretty much a guarantee that Sara would be the first person chosen for most teams. She could hurl a dodge ball with major league pitching speed and shoot a basketball over the outstretched arms of any opponent. CoraLee had quickly snatched Sara up as her three-legged race partner, figuring Sara was such a good athlete that they'd be sure to win. But as EJ watched the two girls practice for the three-legged race, she thought they looked more like a newborn giraffe trying to take its first awkward steps than two girls tied together at the knees.

"Put your arm around my shoulder—like this." Macy took EJ's left arm and draped it around her own shoulder. "And I'll put my right arm over your shoulder. That'll help us stay together even more."

"How do you know so much about three-legged races?" EJ asked. "Is this a secret gymnastics event I've never seen at one of your competitions?" Macy had taken gymnastic lessons since she was three and was really good. EJ had taken six weeks of lessons when she was three until the teacher suggested to Mom that EJ should try doing something that didn't require balance or coordination.

Macy laughed. "No, we don't do three-legged races, but one time we did a team-building exercise where we tied our ankles to someone else's, and we all had to get through an obstacle course. We weren't quite as graceful that day as you'd expect a team of gymnasts to be, that's for sure."

"Like a gymnast centipede—all tied together in a line?" EJ asked, imagining a multilegged gymnast trying to walk across a balance beam.

"Exactly," Macy said. "Compared to that, this race will be a piece of cake."

Macy and EJ practiced walking together, first slowly as Macy called out, "Out, in, out, in!" taking steps with their outside legs and then inside legs at the same time. Pretty soon they were able to start jogging, and then they even sprinted a few steps. The pair ended their practice at the starting line just as Ms. P blew her whistle and told everyone to take their marks.

There were about a dozen teams lined up for the race, everyone looking mildly uncomfortable at being tied to someone else. CoraLee and Sara were directly to their right, the girls arguing over how to call out instructions to each other during the race.

"It needs to be 'right, left,' " CoraLee insisted. "For crying out loud, Sara! Just follow me and let me do it!"

"CoraLee." Sara's voice sounded strained, like she was trying her best to be patient with her partner. "Your *right* leg is tied to my *left* leg, so we need to move our *opposite* legs at the same time or we will end up in a heap on the ground."

EJ tried to hide a grin and focused back on Macy and the race.

"We got this, Mace," EJ said, holding up her palm toward her best friend.

"We got this, EJ," Macy replied, slapping EJ's hand in a high five.

"Ready?" Ms. P called out. "Steady! Go!"

At the sound of Ms. P's whistle, everyone bolted forward—five of the teams falling flat on their faces. For a split second, the arms and legs flailing around EJ made her forget which leg to move first, but she felt Macy's confident step tug on her inside leg, and she heard Macy's clear voice shout, "In! Out! In! Out!" and they took off, quickly falling in step with each other.

EJ saw CoraLee and Sara out of the corner of her eye—Sara picking up CoraLee by the waist after they had fallen to the ground with their first step.

"Arrrgggghhh!" CoraLee let out a frustrated part-scream-part-grunt that sounded to EJ like the sound a baby giraffe might make. . . .

The baby giraffe takes another loping step, finally finding its footing, and lurches forward into an awkward run. Looking around frantically, the gangly creature searches for its mother, but she is nowhere to be found.

"Aww, what a cute little giraffe," EJ said dreamily, looking over her shoulder at CoraLee and Sara. "But where'd the mom go?"

"Come on—they're gaining on us!" Macy said, shaking EJ by the shoulder. "Stay with me, EJ!"

EJ blinked her eyes rapidly to try to keep the daydream from taking over. *Focus, EJ—Macy's counting on you!* she told herself.

"Out! In! Out! In!" EJ fell in step with Macy, and they started gaining speed. Twenty yards from the finish line. . .fifteen yards. . .

EJ took a quick peek to her right and left and didn't see any of the other teams in her line of vision. Were they really going to win the race this easily?

A second later, CoraLee and Sara came out of nowhere and caught up to Macy and EJ. EJ couldn't imagine that they had so quickly figured out how to work together as a team, but then she saw how it happened: Sara's arms were around CoraLee's waist, and the taller girl was literally *carrying* her partner to the finish line.

EJ had to admit Sara's athletic ability was pretty impressive right now.

"Hey, no fair!" EJ shouted, still keeping in step with Macy. "That's cheating!"

"Says who?" CoraLee hissed at EJ. "Get outta the way, EJ Payne-in-my-neck!" CoraLee stuck her foot out just enough to trip EJ's outside leg.

EJ put her free hand out just in time to catch herself from taking a face plant in the grass. In the same moment, she saw that CoraLee's foot had gotten tangled up with Sara's foot and they were falling forward, too.

EJ lifted her head and saw that the finish line was just a few feet ahead of them.

"Macy! Tuck and roll!" she shouted.

With the skill of a pro gymnast, Macy dropped her shoulder toward EJ and propelled herself forward in a burst of speed and power that rolled EJ forward as well. Time seemed to stand still for a moment.

"EJ and Macy—winners!" Ms. P shouted, tweeting her whistle.

Flat on their backs, EJ and Macy looked up at the sky, trying to catch their breath.

"Mace?"

"Yeah?"

"I never thought I'd say this," EJ said, rising up on her elbows. "But that finish was better than anything even my imagination could've come up with."

Chapter 2

Dessert duels

Dear Diary,

Mom is taking Isaac and me grocery shopping in a few minutes.

There are two B words I use to describe grocery shopping: BLEH and BORING.

I would pretty much rather be doing anything else— like reading a good book or playing fetch with Bert in the backyard with his favorite slobbery tennis ball or even helping Mom weed the flower bed (a chore I usually loathe, but right now it sounds better than grocery shopping).

 The only thing that makes this shopping trip not completely terrible is that we're buying food for my birthday party: Mom's homemade lasagna, garlic bread, and salad—and my birthday cake!

Speaking of cake, Mom and I have started watching a TV show called *Dessert Duels*. It's where bakers compete to make the most delicious and best-looking desserts (cakes, cookies, brownies, crème brûlée—you name it!) and a winner is named at the end of every episode.

I don't mean to brag or anything, but I have some pretty amazing baking skills myself. Dad taught me the Payne family recipe for cowboy cookies when I was eight, so I've been perfecting that delicious snack for almost three years now. And I make a mean pan of peanut butter brownies, thanks to lessons from Mom. So count on it, Diary—someday I'll make a winning appearance on *Dessert Duels!*

Mom's yelling up the stairs that it's time to go to the store.

Again, I say: BLEH!

EJ

EJ pressed her nose against the bakery display case and exhaled, admiring the foggy circle her hot breath made on the glass. Scanning the rows of desserts, she quickly spotted a square tray filled with a dozen delicious-looking chocolate cupcakes topped with mounds of fluffy, white frosting and multicolored star sprinkles. EJ pulled her face away from the glass and turned toward Mom, who was reading the nutrition label on a loaf of Italian bread a few feet away.

"Mom, those cupcakes would be *perfect* for my birthday," EJ said, pointing to the star-sprinkled beauties. "Could we get them for my party? Please?"

Mom added the loaf of bread to the shopping basket hanging from the crook of her arm and leaned down next to EJ to get a better look at the cupcakes.

"Those are definitely EJ Payne cupcakes—stars and all," Mom said, smiling. "I admire a woman who knows what she wants."

"May I help you with something, ma'am?" The voice came from behind the display case—a teenage boy with short, dark hair, freckles across his cheeks, and braces. He was wearing a yellow polo shirt with the bakery's logo on the chest: SALLY'S SWEET SHOPPE. Underneath that was a name tag with his name: TROY.

"We're interested in these cupcakes, Troy," Mom said, tapping the glass. "Can you tell me how much they are?"

"Sure thing." Troy slid open a door in the back of the display case, pulled out the tray of cupcakes, and set it on top. "These Chocolate Dream cupcakes are some of Sally's bestsellers."

"I can see why," Mom said, admiring the beautiful colors. "They're gorgeous."

EJ carefully holds the biggest Chocolate Dream cupcake in her hand and admires its perfection for just a moment before pulling away the silvery paper baking cup from the bottom of the cake. She sinks her teeth into the delectable sugary goodness of the frosting and the crunch of the sprinkles as she savors the bite. She looks around at her birthday party guests: Dad and Mr. Johnson both laugh good-naturedly as Isaac's cupcake-eating technique results in a white goatee (with a few sprinkles for added color). Seeing his chance to get some sugar for himself, Bert hops up on the chair next to Isaac and starts licking the frosting from her brother's face while Isaac giggles. Mom and Mrs. Winkle gush over how the cupcakes are almost too pretty to eat (but that won't stop them!). Nana and Pops, arms entwined, romantically feed each other bites of cake. (Gross.) And all thanks to EJ—who picked them out herself!

"And they taste even better than they look, if you can believe it." Troy's voice jolted EJ back to reality in Sally's Sweet Shoppe. "These cupcakes are part of our gourmet line of desserts, and they're. . ." He paused to check a price list behind the counter. "Five fifty each—plus tax."

EJ's stomach dropped to her toes. Five dollars and fifty cents apiece? She did a quick calculation in her head: eight partygoers multiplied by $5.50 was more than $40! EJ knew Mom would never pay that much for a birthday dessert, no matter how amazingly spectacular and perfect it was. Still, she couldn't help but hold out a tiny bit of hope.

"Thanks for your help, Troy." Mom laid a reassuring hand on EJ's shoulder. "We'll talk about it."

EJ knew "We'll talk about it" was Mom language for "No." She sighed and took one last longing glance at the cupcakes as Troy slid them back into their spot behind the glass.

"But, Mom—" EJ started, feeling the sting of disappointed tears well up. Mom hugged EJ around her shoulders.

"Come on, Isaac, we're checking out," Mom called to EJ's little brother, who was near the cookies, trying to convince the teenage girl behind the counter that he couldn't decide which he liked better—the peanut butter or the chocolate chip—so could he please try one more sample of each? If Isaac had another thirty seconds, his six-year-old boy charm might have gotten him not just a taste but an entire cookie. Or maybe even a dozen. The kid knew how to work it.

"Isaac, we're leaving," Mom said in a firmer voice this time. Reluctantly, Isaac walked toward Mom and EJ at the end of a short line at the checkout, shoving a last-second oatmeal cookie sample in his mouth.

"I'm coming, Marm!" Isaac said around a mouthful of cookie. He "helpfully" took the shopping basket from Mom and started swinging it on his arm like a pendulum in a clock.

"Careful, buddy," Mom said, placing a hand on top of his head to keep him contained. "Not too high."

"I gotta burn off that sugar I ate," he said, echoing words he often heard from Mom and Dad. "Or I'll go into HYPERdrive."

EJ could almost see the sugar energy from the cookies coursing through her little brother's arms and legs. Sure, he was naturally already a spaz, but he could usually contain his spazzy-ness to a minimum—especially in public.

"Hey, hyper-driver," EJ said to the basket-swinging Isaac, "I'd like to see what you'd be like after eating one of those Chocolate Dream cupcakes."

Isaac's basket stopped swinging, and his eyes widened with

excitement at the thought. "I would be. . .unstoppable," he whispered in awe.

Mom laughed as they moved forward in the checkout line.

"On second thought," EJ said, imagining an unstoppably hyper Isaac, "I think you should only be allowed that much sugar if we have a padded room to lock you in for the next six hours."

"Are we going to get those cupcakes for EJ's birthday?" Isaac asked, switching up his basket antics by raising and lowering it by the handle in a bicep curl.

"Those Chocolate Dream cupcakes *are* pretty spectacular," Mom said, looking over her shoulder toward the cake display.

"Yeah, but I know they're too expensive," EJ said, studying the tiles on the floor.

"They are too expensive; you're right," Mom said, sounding almost as disappointed as EJ felt. "But you know, I don't think they're actually special enough for your eleventh birthday, EJ." Mom took the basket from Isaac and placed the two loaves of Italian bread and a tub of garlic butter on the counter for the cashier to ring up.

EJ squinted at Mom, looking unsure. What could be better than chocolate cupcakes with star sprinkles?

"What if we make our own cupcakes?" Mom suggested, a sly twinkle in her eye. "*Dessert Duels* style. EJ versus Mom."

Isaac spun around from where he had been poking the side of a plastic-wrapped angel food cake and watching the dent spring back to its original shape. "Like a food fight?" he asked.

"Not throwing food but more of a food throw-down. Then the party guests could be the judges," Mom said as she swiped her debit card through the machine. "What do you think, birthday girl?"

EJ closed her eyes and tried to imagine the best cupcakes ever: chocolate. . .no, devil's food. And cream-filled centers! With triple-fudge icing and sparkly gold flecks that reflected in the light—and multicolored star-shaped sprinkles!

EJ opened her eyes wide and grinned. "Could I decorate my cupcakes however I want? Even better than the Chocolate Dream ones?" she asked.

"It's your birthday—do it up right!" Mom said.

"Where's my favorite set of measuring cups?"

Chef EJ looks frantically amid the clutter of ingredients on the stainless-steel countertop for the set of red plastic measuring cups—her good luck charm during baking competitions.

"Right here, chef!" EJ's kitchen assistant, Isaac, pops up from under the counter and hands her the cups.

"Isaac, were these on the floor?" EJ asks, inspecting the measuring cups for any sign of dirt.

"Yes, chef," Isaac says matter-of-factly, "but they didn't break the five-second rule. And it's a scientific fact that when something falls on the floor, it doesn't get dirty until it's been there for at least five seconds!"

Although the logic seems iffy to EJ, she doesn't have time to argue. "Thank you, Isaac," she says, picking up the recipe card to see what she needs to do next.

"Time to mix up the cream for the cupcake centers!" Chef EJ flashes a winning smile and a thumbs-up toward camera two just before the announcer takes Dessert Duels *to a commercial break.*

"Who will control this epic battle for dessert dominance? The fifteen-year cupcake veteran, Chef Tabby? Or the newbie, Chef EJ?" the

deep male voice asks the unseen TV audience on the other side of the camera. "We'll be right back after these commercial messages."

"EJ, you're doing great!" Mom said, scooping vanilla cupcake batter into a cupcake pan. "I'm proud of you!"

"Thanks, Mom." EJ smiled, unaware that she had a streak of flour smeared across her forehead. "This is so fun. I'm sorry I'm going to have to beat you in the final judging. Who in their right mind is going to pick a vanilla cupcake over a chocolate cream-filled one?"

"You're right," Mom said, licking a dab of batter off her thumb. "I stand no chance."

Isaac appeared between Mom and EJ. "And we're back from commercial in three. . .two. . .one."

Chef EJ glances over her shoulder at the digital countdown on the wall. Four minutes and eight seconds left. Time to shift into high gear to get her cupcakes in the oven before time runs out.

"Eight ounces of soft cream cheese, one-quarter cup cocoa powder, and a half cup of sugar," EJ mutters, reading off the recipe card. She quickly adds the first two ingredients to the glass mixing bowl, but when she reaches for the sugar, it's not there.

"Isaac!" A tone of urgency is in her voice. "Isaac! Sugar?"

Suddenly she spots a plastic bowl filled with white granules sitting on top of the stove. "Never mind—found it!" EJ quickly shoves the half-cup measuring cup in the bowl and scoops out a level measure before dumping it into the mixing bowl and flipping the mixer's switch to the ON position.

"Hurry, Chef EJ. . .just three minutes left!" the announcer voice annoyingly reminds her.

"Where's that assistant of mine?" Chef EJ looks around for Isaac.

"May I help?"

EJ looks up from the chocolate cream mixing in front of her to see her competitor—Chef Tabby—holding a cupcake pan in one hand and a sleeve of cupcake liners in the other.

"You want to help me?" Chef EJ can hardly believe what she's hearing. "But we're trying to beat each other! You know, the 'epic battle for dessert dominance'?"

"Well, my cupcakes are already in the oven, and it looks like you could use a little help." Chef Tabby sets the pan on the counter and places a liner in each of the dozen cupcake wells.

"Sure. That's—uh—great. Thank you," Chef EJ stammers as she tries to remain focused. "Put in one scoop of cake batter for each of the cupcakes," she says, handing Chef Tabby an ice-cream scoop, and then adds, "please."

"Right away, chef!" Tabby grins and salutes EJ with the scoop before getting to work.

"Ninety seconds!" the announcer voice says.

"Yeah, GOT IT!" Chef EJ yells back.

EJ turns off the mixer and removes the glass bowl just as Chef Tabby finishes adding the last of the batter to the pan. EJ spoons a dollop of cream filling on top of the batter of each cupcake.

"Oven is preheated to three fifty and ready to go, chef!" Tabby calls from the oven across the kitchen.

As she finishes the final dollop, EJ glances over the entire pan, pleased with the result. She closes her eyes and can already imagine what will come out of the oven: perfectly rounded domes of devil's food hiding the surprise centers of heavenly chocolate cream. Her mouth starts to water.

"Chef! Ten seconds!" Tabby's voice wakes EJ from her vision. "Nine. . .eight. . ."

EJ grabs the cupcake pan with two hands and runs toward the oven. One step, two steps.

"Five. . .four. . ." Chef Tabby counts with the clock, opening the oven door as EJ sprints her way.

Three steps, four steps—EJ reaches as far as she can to slide the cupcake pan into the oven. Tabby slams the door just as the clock reaches zero.

"Well done, chef," Mom said, grabbing the wet dishcloth from the sink and wiping the flour from EJ's forehead. "The judges are going to have a difficult time deciding a winner."

Chapter 3

The Mysterious Case of

the Birthday Barfs

Dear Diary,

Today is my eleventh birthday, and tonight is my par-tay! Mom and Mrs. Winkle have been super secretive about the details of the mystery dinner theater, but I know it will be awesome because it's going to include people I love (family and friends), the food I love (lasagna and my award-winning cupcakes), and the things I love (we're all going to be acting out a whodunit mystery during the party)!

The one thing I do know about the mystery setup is that I will be playing the part of detective EJ Holmes. I'm still working on my costume, but Mr. Johnson let me borrow a magnifying glass he uses when he works on his stamp collection. The thing is legit.

Nana and Pops arrived from Ohio in their Winnebago camper late last night. Mom and Dad let us stay up till they got here, but it was so late that Isaac and I both fell asleep on the couch. ALL I really remember was (sort of) waking up when Pops picked me up to carry me to my bed. And I was just wrapping my arms around Pops's neck to give him a squeeze hello when I heard my brother wake up in classic Isaac style:

Isaac: [yawning] Knock-knock, Pops.
Pops: Who's there, sport?
Isaac: Noah.
Pops: Noah who?
Isaac: Noah. . .good. . .joke? [snore]
Pops: [chuckling to himself] No, Isaac, I don't Noah good joke. You know the only good one.

(I've really got to get that kid some new material.)
                    EJ

EJ pulled the deerstalker cap down on her forehead, held the magnifying glass up to her right eye, and peered at herself in the mirror on the back of her bedroom door.

"Quite good," she said in her best British accent. "EJ Holmes, consulting detective, ready for a birthday mystery."

EJ tied a tweed cape around her neck and glanced over her shoulder at Bert, who was sprawled on her bed. "Watson, old chap, come here for your costume," she said, tucking the magnifying glass in the cape's inside pocket.

Bert gave a little snort and didn't move.

"Watson, I said come here," EJ insisted.

Bert rolled over and stretched, his back toward EJ.

"Matthew Cuthbert T-Rex Payne, *come*!"

(EJ rarely used Bert's full name—including the "T-Rex" part that Isaac gave him—unless she really meant business.)

Bert was up like a flash and next to EJ, on his back legs with his paws on her leg. EJ smiled and patted her friend on his furry head. "I guess you're not used to being called Watson, huh? I'm Sherlock Holmes, and you're my partner, John Watson. And it's time for your costume."

EJ plopped a dog-size bowler hat on Bert's head, adjusting the band of elastic around his ears and under his chin. Attached to the brim of the hat was a monocle that rested perfectly against his snout and in front of his right eye.

"You look splendid, Dr. Watson!" EJ picked Bert up and looked in the mirror again to get the full effect.

"Miss Holmes and Dr. Watson, so good of you to join us!" Mom greeted EJ and Bert at the bottom of the stairs a few minutes later.

Mom looked like she'd stepped right out of the 1920s, wearing a sleeveless purple-sequined flapper dress, her long blond hair in curls that were held back from her face by a headband made out of black feathers. Mom glanced down at the note card she had in her hand before continuing. "My name is Penny Pickpocket, and I am your hostess for tonight's dinner. May I take your hats?"

EJ tried to stay in character, but she couldn't help but crack a smile at Mom's character name. She wasn't going to let somebody with the last name of *Pickpocket* take anything of hers.

"Thank you, Penny, but I think we'll keep our hats on," EJ said, stooping to pat Bert on his bowler hat. "It's part of the look we're going for, right, Watson?"

Bert barked his agreement and ran in a circle next to EJ.

"Let me introduce you to everyone," Mom said, putting one hand on EJ's shoulder to direct her into the living room. EJ felt Mom's other hand slip into her Sherlock cape pocket.

"Excuse me, Miss Pickpocket." EJ spun around to see Mom staring through the magnifying glass at EJ with an innocent look on her face. "That's mine. And I think you should keep your sticky fingers to yourself, Penny."

"Sorry about that, but I know someone who would pay top dollar for a fine tool like this." Mom's magnified eye winked at EJ before she handed the glass back to her. "And it's *Mrs.* Pickpocket. Allow me to introduce my husband, Peter Pickpocket."

Dad stepped forward and caught EJ's right hand in a firm two-handed shake. "We've heard so much about your mystery-solving abilities, Miss Holmes. Although, as you can see, none of us are shady characters, so hopefully we will just have a nice dinner together."

Dad was wearing a rumpled brown suit, slicked-back hair, and fake gold rings on most of his fingers—definitely a shady character in EJ's mind. She glanced down at her wrist to check the time, only to find her watch was missing.

"Looking for something, Holmes?"

EJ looked up to see Dad holding her wristwatch by its leather strap.

"The closure must've been loose," Dad said, handing the watch back to EJ and running his hand through his hair. "It slipped right into my hand."

"Quite a coincidence," EJ said, squinting at Dad in a skeptical look. She pulled a tiny spiral notebook and pencil out of her cape and made a note:

1.   Penny and Peter Pickpocket: steal things to sell for profit.

Next Mom introduced Nana and Pops as Victoria and Richard Rich, an extremely wealthy couple visiting from the East.

"Don't you just *love* the way diamonds add sparkle to any outfit, darling?" Nana was really playing up the part of a rich lady, admiring the big, phony diamonds on her rings and in the multiple strands of diamonds around her neck.

"I wouldn't know, Mrs. Rich," EJ said. "I've never worn diamonds."

"Oh!" Nana gasped and held the back of her hand to her forehead in a dramatic gesture. "Then you *must* try these on. . .but just for the evening. I'll want them back, of course."

Nana slipped a necklace on her granddaughter's neck. EJ did like how sparkly it was.

"Nothing's too good for my Victoria," Pops said a little stiffly, looking down at his note card. "I want her to be the most beautiful woman in the room, wherever she goes." Pops looked pretty uncomfortable in his special-occasion suit, polished dress shoes, and bowtie.

EJ made another note in her notebook:

2. Victoria and Richard Rich: want to appear to have a lot of money—no matter what.

"I'm William Baker." Mr. Johnson waved from his seat in the recliner. He looked down at his note card before continuing. "I'm about to open up my own bakery in town, and I would really like to get my hands on the cupcakes to see if I can steal the recipe and perfect it for my store."

Mr. Johnson was wearing everyday clothes, with the addition of a leopard-print baker's hat and apron that EJ recognized as a set Mrs. Winkle owned.

"Cupcakes are for dessert, Mr. Baker," Mom said to Mr. Johnson. Then she whispered, "And that part of your card isn't what you're supposed to *say*, Lester. It's supposed to tell you your *motivation* for the mystery."

"My motivation is that I'm starving!" Mr. Johnson grunted.

EJ thought for a moment before adding to her notebook:

3. William Baker: hungry—for food and for his bakery to be a success.

"And this is Wildcard McGee," Mom said as Isaac took a deep bow.

Isaac was wearing green cowboy boots and Mom's white bathrobe with big purple polka dots on it, a Superman cape pinned to the back of the robe. All that was bizarre enough, but what really put the outfit over the top was a pair of costume glasses with a fake nose, mustache, and eyebrows attached.

"Great to meet you, Holmes." Isaac grabbed EJ's hand and started pumping her arm like he was trying to bring water up from a well in an old-timey movie. "Do you have any spare acorn tops on you this evening?"

"Acorn tops? Um—no, I'm afraid I'm fresh out," EJ said, not sure what to make of this strange character.

EJ quickly jotted another note:

4. Wildcard McGee: ???

"No problem. I have an extra acorn top you can borrow." Isaac reached into his pocket and pulled out the part of an acorn that looks like a little hat and dropped it into EJ's outstretched hand. "Now, do this." Isaac took out a second acorn top, held it between his thumbs and pointer fingers and blew into it, causing an ear-piercing whistle that made everyone in the room wince and plug their ears. Bert, who looked like he wished he could cover his ears but couldn't, joined in the noise by howling at a similar pitch.

"And that *delightful* sound must mean dinner is served!" Mrs. Winkle said as she entered the living room. She was wearing a flouncy apron with pink and purple swirls all over it and had a pair of tongs in her hand.

"Miss Holmes, I'm Cookie Cookson, and I had the distinct pleasure of preparing tonight's meal for us to enjoy." Mrs. Winkle hugged EJ in a very Mrs. Winkle-y warm way and then added with a little edge to her voice, "Well, I prepared all but the dessert. Apparently *some people* think my baking skills aren't good enough for the occasion."

"If everyone would follow me into the dining area, we'll get the meal under way," Mom said, ushering the guests into the kitchen and eyeballing Nana's diamonds with a wistful look in her eye.

EJ made another note as she followed the group to the table:

5.   Cookie Cookson: bitter about not getting to make dessert.

"Cookie, you have really outdone yourself this time." Mr. Johnson wiped his mouth with his napkin, which was tucked into the top of his apron. "Now, where is that dessert I heard about?"

Mrs. Winkle blushed at the compliment from Mr. Johnson before remembering to stay in character. "Oh, right. . .the dessert," she said in an annoyed voice. "The cupcakes for tonight's dessert were baked by two celebrity chefs, and we're going to vote to choose a winner."

There was a murmuring of interest around the table as Mrs. Winkle rose to get the dessert.

"No matter what, I'm voting chocolate," EJ said, obviously trying to influence the vote.

"But sometimes vanilla really hits the spot," Mom chimed in, playing the same game as EJ.

"Without any further ado, I give you Chef EJ's Dreamstar Cupcakes and Chef Tabby's Heaven-Sent Cupcakes!" Mrs. Winkle set a cake stand in the middle of the table and lifted the silver dome to reveal. . .

An empty tray.

"*Nobody move!*" *EJ Holmes jumps up from her seat, magnifying glass in hand. "This is a crime scene, and you're all guilty until I've proven you innocent!"*

The guests look suspiciously at each other as EJ stands on her chair to inspect the empty cake stand.

"*Aha! A clue!*" *EJ picks up a photo on the tray and peers at it through her magnifying class: a dozen beautiful cupcakes displayed on the cake stand—six devil's food with fudge frosting, multicolored star-shaped sprinkles, and sparkle flecks, and six white cake with fluffy white frosting topped with a sprinkling of gorgeous edible pearls.*

"*One of you has stolen these delicious desserts, and it's my job to find out who—and why.*" *EJ Holmes steps off the chair and walks around the table, looking at each suspect—one at a time—through the magnifying glass.*

"*William Baker,*" *EJ says, consulting her notes. "Your business depends on getting the very best baked goods to sell in your store. You had the motive to steal these cupcakes to uncover the secret recipes.*"

"*I don't need to be some copycat!*" *William protests. "My baked goods are better than any that are out there!"*

"*Then there's Mr. and Mrs. Pickpocket.*" *EJ moves down the table. "They would've seen the business potential of stealing some delicious cupcakes and then selling them to the highest bidder.*"

Penny and Peter look shocked at the accusation.

"*Or maybe you two have sticky fingers because you both have a sweet tooth, and you stole the cupcakes to eat them yourselves!*" *EJ adds.*

"*I admit those cupcakes do look mighty fancy,*" *Peter says. "But we deal only in precious metals, Miss Holmes. Gold. Silver. Jewels. Things that are worth real money.*"

"In that case"—EJ glances at her notes and moves on to the next suspects—"Mr. Rich, you said you always want your wife to be the most beautiful woman in the room, no matter where she goes. Perhaps the cupcakes were outshining your wife, so you had to get rid of them!"

"Oh, don't be silly, Miss Holmes," Victoria Rich says, twisting a strand of pearls around her finger. "Those cupcakes are a poor man's idea of wealth next to my sparkle. By the way, I'd like my diamonds back now."

"I don't like how they feel on my skin anyway. Here you go." EJ removes the diamond strand from her neck and hands it back to Mrs. Rich.

"This never would've happened if I'd been allowed to make the dessert," Cookie says, crossing her arms in disgust. "Celebrity chefs are all divas, and their fancy-pants desserts cause nothing but trouble."

"And maybe, Cookie, just maybe. . .you stole the cupcakes to make your point!" EJ says, pointing her magnifying glass at Cookie with a dramatic flair.

"I most certainly did not," Cookie says. "No matter how much I may dislike another chef, I would never sabotage her work. That is downright unprofessional."

"Then, of course! Why didn't I see it before?" EJ Holmes is desperate to figure out who is guilty. "Wildcard McGee must be guilty of the crime!" EJ looks at her notebook. "Except. . .well, to be honest, Wildcard, I have no idea who you are or what your motivation for stealing the cupcakes might be."

"Because they are fun to throw in food fights!" Wildcard wiggles his eyebrows, causing his glasses/nose/mustache to move up and down on his face, making him look even sillier. "If I stole them, we'd all be covered in cake, frosting, and sprinkles right now."

EJ scratches her head with her magnifying glass and looks down at her notes. Not one of her suspects is guilty. Some detective she is turning out to be.

"Watson, what do you think?" EJ Holmes glances down at the floor. "Watson? Has anybody seen Watson?"

EJ kneels on the floor to search for her missing friend. Looking through the magnifying glass, she spies Watson's dog dish in the corner, empty.

"Cookie, did you feed Watson at the same time you served our dinner tonight?" EJ asks.

"Not my department," Cookie says, annoyed. "I feed people, not animals."

Suddenly there is a scratching sound at the pantry door, followed by a sharp bark that EJ immediately recognizes as none other than. . .

"Watson stole the cupcakes!" EJ announced triumphantly as she opened the pantry door to find Bert inside, along with the tray of cupcakes. Bert jumped into EJ's arms, his tail wagging as he licked her face.

Everyone at the table burst into applause and echoed a chorus of "Well done!" and "Good job!" EJ grinned and took a bow with Bert still in her arms.

"Watson, how could you betray me for a life of crime?" she asked Bert teasingly.

"To be fair to Bert, we did set him up," Mom said as she set the tray of cupcakes on the table. "Did you figure out *why* Watson stole the cupcakes?"

"Elementary, my dear mother!" EJ said in a British accent. "We didn't feed him, so he stole the cupcakes because he was hungry."

"Speaking of hungry, are we going to eat this delicious dessert or not?" asked Mr. Johnson.

"First we light candles and sing, Lester!" Mrs. Winkle chided him.

Mom and Mrs. Winkle made quick work of adding eleven birthday candles to the cupcakes and setting them ablaze. Pops's deep singing voice led everyone in "Happy Birthday."

EJ closed her eyes, made a wish, and blew out all the candles on her first try. Everyone clapped, and Isaac called out, "Food fight!" and made a lunge for the cupcakes.

"Nice try, Wildcard." Dad grabbed him by the Superman cape and stopped him midair. "Maybe we'll have a food fight on *your* birthday."

"But don't count on it," Mom added.

"Okay, on to the judging," Mrs. Winkle said. On her cue, everyone took a bite of Mom's Heaven-Sent Cupcakes.

EJ had to admit it was pretty amazing.

"Oh honey, it's like a fluffy cloud in my mouth!" Dad said. "In the best way possible, of course."

"Light as a feather," Nana said, smiling. "I've taught you well, Tabby."

Mom beamed and said, "Let's see if I've done as good a job in teaching my daughter as you've taught me."

EJ peeled back the paper liner of her cupcake and took one last admiring look at the perfectly piped chocolate frosting, edible gold flecks, and multicolored sprinkles before taking a giant bite of her cupcake. . .

. . .a bite she immediately regretted.

Maybe I just got a dud, EJ thought as she tried to choke down the disgusting bite of cake. *My perfect Dreamstar Cupcakes can't all be this bad. . . .*

"BLECH!" EJ looked up to see Isaac spit out his cupcake onto Mr. Johnson's napkin bib.

In one fluid motion—even faster than Mr. Johnson could react—Mom responded by scooping up the napkin and cake spit on Mr. Johnson's chest and removing them from sight.

"That cupcake was Nasty McNasterson!" Isaac yelled, confirming what EJ feared: her cupcakes were terrible. She felt the sting of disappointed tears in her eyes, and her stomach lurched in embarrassment.

EJ searched the faces around the table to find looks of disgust—not just at Isaac's display of bad table manners but obviously because they wished they could spit out the cupcake like Isaac had just done. Pops looked like he was trying to will himself to chew once, twice—enough to somehow swallow the tragedy in his mouth. Mrs. Winkle was fanning her face with her hand, her cheeks bulging with inedible cake. Dad gulped some water to try to dilute the taste in his mouth and patted his belly, trying (unsuccessfully) to convince EJ it was the best thing he'd ever eaten.

She knew there was only one way to end this cake standoff, so she picked up her napkin and deposited her mouthful of putrid dessert into it.

"Nobody has to eat these," EJ announced.

The adults around the table plastered painful-looking smiles on their faces and shrugged their shoulders, which EJ interpreted as "Oh, it's not so bad," and "I think if I just try another bite, the taste will grow on me."

Isaac looked around at the faces and said, "EJ, you think *I'm* crazy, but they are the crazy ones! Your cupcakes are *awful!*"

"I *know*, Isaac!" EJ hissed at her brother, embarrassed heat rising in her cheeks. "Why do you think I spit mine out?"

EJ watched the faces around the table start to turn a particularly sick shade of green. She appreciated that everyone was trying to make her feel okay about her cupcakes, but enough was enough.

"Seriously, everyone. I don't care that it's my birthday. So, please," she pleaded. "Spit. It. Out!"

There was a moment when the adults looked at EJ to make sure she was really okay with what was about to happen. Seeing their hesitation, EJ nodded, and then there was a collective sigh of relief as everyone spit cake into their napkins.

"Oh EJ!" Mrs. Winkle said after taking a drink of water. "I have to give you some credit for such a *spectacularly* terrible cupcake."

EJ smiled to herself, and her embarrassment began to melt away. Mrs. Winkle always knew how to find the bright side of every situation.

"It tasted like the bottom of a shoe after a walk on the beach," Dad said, using a spoon to scrape the taste out of his mouth. "Salty and gritty. Any idea how you managed that, EJ?"

"I followed the recipe." EJ shrugged. "Maybe it was sabotaged."

"Maybe, but you're competing against your mom," Dad said. "She likes to win almost as much as you do, but I don't think she's so competitive that she would ruin her own daughter's cupcakes."

"Um, EJ," Mom called from inside the pantry. "Where did you get the sugar you used for the cupcakes?"

"From a plastic bowl with sugar in it," she said, envisioning the bowl she had found on the stovetop.

"That's what I was afraid of," Mom said, emerging from the

pantry with the bowl in her hands. "It's not sugar. It's salt I use for cleaning the copper bottoms of my pots. I must've left it out last time I was cleaning!"

"Mystery number two of the evening, solved," EJ said, raising the magnifying glass to her eye. "Next time I need a Watson, you're my man—er—woman, Mom."

Chapter 4

THEM ALL (OF AMERICA)

Dear Diary,

Reason 648 to love summer vacation: road trips!

Nana and Pops are taking Isaac, Bert, and me on an overnight trip to Minneapolis. I'm writing this diary entry from the comfy couch in their Winnebago, the Wisconsin countryside speeding by outside the window. Pops is behind the wheel, singing an eighteenth verse of "Down by the Bay" at the top of his lungs while Bert sits in the co-captain seat, howling along at the "back to my home, I dare not goooooo" part. (Bert likes to think of himself as a world-famous opera singer. So what if he is a dog?) Nana and Isaac are sitting at the kitchenette table playing "I Spy," and Isaac is definitely winning. I'm pretty sure he's cheating, because he keeps making up names of colors. (I just heard him say, "I spy something greepurlow," which I'm guessing is green, purple, and yellow.) But Nana seems to be playing along, so maybe the names of colors have changed since I was in kindergarten.

If you ask me, this is a pretty great way to travel.

The plans for today include  spending the afternoon at the Mall of America. To be honest, Diary, I was a little nervous when Nana said we were going to spend most of the day at a mall. (I mean, you and I both know how I feel about shopping.) But apparently there is a LOT more to do at this mall than just shop—like an aquarium, a movie theater, miniature golf, and even an indoor amusement park.

That sounds like my kind of shopping.

EJ

EJ closed her diary before stretching out on the small couch.

"Hey, Pops, can I ask you something?" she called up to her grandpa, who was expertly driving the camper down the highway.

"Anything, DG," Pops said. EJ loved it when he called her DG—short for "dear granddaughter." He smiled at her in the rearview mirror. "Ask away!"

"How many verses of 'Down by the Bay' are there?" she asked, grinning.

"Not enough!" Pops replied, knowing EJ was teasing him about his never-ending singing. "Let's come up with a few more."

"Have you already done 'Did you ever see a bear combing his hair?' " EJ asked.

"Please, do I look like an amateur?" Pops said. "That's the very first verse Bert and I sang."

"How about 'a llama wearing his pajamas'?" EJ asked.

"Yep, did that one, too," Pops said. "Come on—give me something new to inspire me."

EJ thought for a moment, but nothing came to mind.

"Did you ever see a dino, falling on his spine-o?" Isaac laughed like it was the most hilarious thing he'd ever said.

"Spine-o? Really?" EJ rolled her eyes.

"Now there's a fantastic verse to add to the mix, sport," Pops said, chuckling. "Here we go. Altogether now—" Pops began to sing at the top of his lungs:

Pops: Down by the bay. . .
Nana and Isaac: Down by the bay. . .
Pops: Where the watermelons grow. . .
Nana and Isaac: Where the watermelons grow. . .

"Can't hear you, EJ!" Pops said. "Come on, now. Without you, our four-part harmony is a sad three."

Bert yipped and glared at Pops.

"Oh right. My apologies, Bertie," Pops said to the pup. "*Five*-part harmony."

"All right, all right," EJ said, giving in. "Just so you know, I'm singing under protest that *spine-o* isn't an actual word."

Pops winked at EJ in the rearview mirror, cleared his throat, and picked up where he left off:

Pops: Back to my home. . .
Nana, Isaac, and EJ: Back to my home. . .
Pops: I dare not goooooo!
Nana, Isaac, and EJ: I dare not goooooo! (**Bert:** Ooooooo!)
Pops: For if I do. . .
Nana, Isaac, and EJ: For if I do. . .
Pops: My mother will say. . .
Nana, Isaac, and EJ: My mother will say. . .
Everybody: Did you ever see a dino, falling on his spine-o—down by the bay?

Fifteen minutes later, after they'd gone through about a dozen new verses (EJ's favorite was "Did you ever see a possum doing something awesome?"), Isaac asked, "Who are we going to see when we get to America?"

Nana looked at EJ with a "Do you know what your brother is talking about?" look. EJ shrugged. She rarely knew what was going on in her brother's head.

"What do you mean 'when we get to America,' sweetie?" Nana

asked Isaac. "We're in America now."

"Well, I *think* we're still in America," Pops said from behind the wheel. "I'm not sure I completely trust the navigation system in this camper. We might actually be in Canada by now."

EJ hoped that meant they'd hear some French-Canadian accents at their next stop. But when she saw the twinkle in Pops's eye, she realized he was just kidding.

"But Mom told me last night at bedtime that you guys were taking me and EJ to America to see them all." EJ could see that Isaac was getting a tiny bit frustrated as he tried to explain himself. "So I want to know who 'them all' is."

"Them all. Them all," Nana repeated the phrase, mulling it over until her face lit up with recognition. "Oh! Isaac! The mall! We're going to the Mall of America! Not 'them all'—it's 'the mall'! Can you hear how they sort of sound the same?"

Isaac nodded, his cheeks and ears turning red. EJ could tell he was embarrassed at his silly mistake. It wasn't like usual when Isaac was being goofy on purpose. This time he actually didn't know what he was saying, and EJ knew this could end badly—maybe in tears. Even though her brother was a Space Invader, she didn't like to see him cry. Without hesitating, EJ started laughing and even threw in a snort for believability.

"Isaac, you really had us going!" EJ said in between fits of laughing, wiping away nonexistent laugh tears from her eyes. "Seriously, kid, you really know how to tell a good joke."

Nana and Pops joined in, laughing. Isaac looked from face to face, not sure at first how to respond, but he quickly brightened and took his cue from EJ's words.

"If you think that joke was good, wait till I pull out the big guns." Isaac grinned a missing-tooth grin. "Knock-knock."

EJ groaned and put a couch pillow over her head.

"The crowd holds its breath while world-famous golfer EJ Payne sizes up the hole. The youngest golfer ever to qualify for a professional tournament, Miss Payne has the eyes of the entire world on her as she takes the most important putt of her career."

"No pressure or anything," EJ mutters to the unseen announcer voice.

"This particular par-four has quite a few tricky obstacles, including banked inclines, two bowling ball–size rocks right down the middle, and a waterfall hazard that could pose a problem for EJ."

EJ gets down on her hands and knees and looks toward the pin. She'll have to hook the ball around the waterfall to reach the hole—a nearly impossible shot for even the most skilled putter.

"No sweat." EJ flashes a winning smile to the spectators as she stands up and grips her putter. "Hey kids, eat a good breakfast and you can be a superstar golfer, too. Watch this."

EJ takes a practice swing with the putter before stepping up to the ball. One last look at the hole and she taps the ball with an expert amount of speed and spin. . .avoiding the inclines. . .past the rocks. . .hooking around the water—

Splash!

"Noooooo!" EJ dropped her golf club, crumpled to her knees, and shook her fists in the air in a display of drama that rivaled any nail-biter on the PGA tour. The sound of the excited screams coming from the indoor roller coaster had jolted her out of her daydream, but she was disappointed in the shot on the Moose Mountain Adventure Golf Course, nonetheless.

"Good job, EJ!" Isaac ran to the base of the waterfall and pointed to EJ's red golf ball at the bottom of the shallow pool. "You got it right in the water!"

"That's not what I was aiming for, Isaac!" EJ wondered if Isaac fully understood the point of golf.

"Aw, that shot looked golden, DG!" Pops retrieved EJ's golf ball from the water and set it on the green so she could take her next shot. "I guess your championship chances are done for today, huh?"

"Yeah." EJ picked up her putter and stood up. "I don't think golf is really my sport."

"The clothes are spectacular," Nana said with a hint of humor in her voice, "but I doubt most courses would let you wear your Converse All-Stars on the greens."

"Deal breaker!" EJ said, smiling. "I never really wanted to be a golfer anyway."

"Pops, it says that the kids' meals are for ages ten and under," EJ said, pointing to the Rainforest Café menu. "Does that mean. . . ?" She let the question hang in the air.

"Well, you're eleven now, DG," Pops said, looking up from his menu and over his reading glasses at EJ. "Looks like you're a full-fledged adult! At least by restaurant standards."

"Yesss!" EJ disappeared behind the menu to concentrate on making the best possible choice.

"I will always want to order from the kids' menu—even when I'm a hundred," Isaac said, drawing with crayons on the jungle-themed kids' menu. "They've got dinosaur-shaped nuggets."

"That *does* seem like a no-brainer, sport," Pops said, smiling. "I wonder if they'll let me order those, too."

"What a fantastic restaurant," Nana said, looking up at the ceiling decorated to look like the tree canopy of a rainforest. "It's like being in the great outdoors without the giant bugs."

"Oooo! Do they have bugs on the menu?" Isaac asked. "Those would go great on top of my dino nuggets!"

Nana pretended to check the menu. "No bugs. Sorry, buddy." Nana didn't sound very sorry.

A perky waitress arrived at the table.

"Hi, I'm Candace, and I'll be taking care of you today," she said, taking a pad of paper and pen out of her apron pocket. "What can I get for you?"

"I'll have the buffalo wings," EJ said decisively, folding the menu and setting it in front of her. "And water to drink, please."

Pops peered at EJ over his reading glasses. "EJ, are you sure you want buffalo wings? The menu says they're spicy."

"Bring it on!" EJ smiled at Pops, licked her lips, and rubbed her hands together. "The spicier the better, I say."

EJ saw Nana and Pops raise their eyebrows at each other.

"Okay, EJ, if you say so," Nana said, shrugging.

Candace took the rest of the orders (a Cobb salad for Nana, a turkey club sandwich for Pops, and dino nuggets with fries for Isaac, water all around), picked up the menus, and left the table.

"So, what's new in the world of my favorite grandkids?" Pops asked, slipping his reading glasses into the chest pocket of his Hawaiian shirt.

"I'm going to day camp with EJ!" Isaac said, bouncing in his chair. "It's going to be the best day this summer!"

"You're not going *with* me," EJ corrected him. "I'm going to be at camp all week, and you're going to come and invade my space for a day."

A genius idea crossed EJ's mind. "Actually, Isaac, you know what would be super fun at day camp?"

"What?" Isaac asked, his eyes bright.

"If you pretend that I'm invisible and I pretend you're invisible!" EJ said, trying her best to sell the plan to her little brother. "You and I would both know that we're there, but everyone else will think that we can't see each other because we're not talking to or even looking at each other!"

"Whoa!" Isaac seemed to like the possibility. "Like a secret mission?"

Nana and Pops chuckled.

"EJ, you really shouldn't tease your brother," Nana said. "There are lots of kids out there who wish they had siblings like you and Isaac."

"Those kids can have him," EJ said under her breath.

"Nana's right," Pops said. "Take me, for example. I was an only child because my parents died in a car accident when I was two."

EJ had heard the story before—how Pops didn't have any relatives who could take him in, so he lived in three different foster homes before he was finally adopted when he was nine.

"But when Great-Grandma and Great-Grandpa Wiley adopted you, you got two older brothers and a little sister," EJ said. "Didn't they ever get on your nerves?"

"Oh, sure. We absolutely annoyed each other. I'm sure they thought I was such a pest sometimes," Pops said, grinning. "But I liked having siblings a lot more than not having siblings."

EJ tried to imagine what it would be like to be an only child.

For the first five years of her life, she had been an only child—but she remembered just bits and pieces of what that was like. Some of her first memories were of being excited that a new baby brother was going to join the family. She even helped Mom decide on decorations for the nursery—a Noah's ark theme. And she remembered picking out a stuffed T-Rex toy especially for the baby before he was born. Isaac still slept with that raggedy T-Rex, missing left eye and all.

"Buffalo chicken wings?" Candace was holding up a large plate of wings in front of EJ's nose.

"Yeah, that's me, thanks." EJ pulled her elbows from the table to make room for the plate. After placing everyone else's food in front of them, Candace said she'd be back in a bit to check on them and walked away.

"Isaac, would you pray for the meal?" Pops asked.

Isaac dropped the Brontosaurus-shaped nugget he was about to stuff into his mouth and nodded solemnly before folding his hands and bowing his head.

"Dear God," Isaac began. "Thank You that Pops has brothers and a sister now, and that he doesn't have to play alone anymore. Thank You, God, that I don't have to play alone either—because You gave me a sister. And also she is fun to bug sometimes."

EJ peeked at Isaac and saw that he was peeking at her, too. They surprised each other and quickly shut their eyes tight. Isaac continued to pray.

"Thank You for Nana and Pops and their sweet Winnebago and this fun trip to see America and the mall, too. Amen."

"And bless this food to our bodies. In Jesus' name, amen." Nana added.

EJ picked up a buffalo wing drumstick and bit into it, immediately feeling the heat of the spicy sauce on her tongue—quite a bit hotter than she'd expected.

Pops saw the shocked expression on EJ's face as she swallowed the first bite of chicken before grabbing her glass of water to take a gulp. "That stuff will put hair on your chest, DG. You sure you can handle it?"

"I'm an adult now, Pops. I order from the adult menu," EJ said, determination in her voice. "I will conquer this plate of buffalo wings if it's the last thing I do."

Then she whispered so only Pops could hear, "Would you get Candace to bring me another glass of water, please?"

The crowded restaurant waits in hushed anticipation while extreme eater EJ Payne mentally prepares for the world record she will attempt to break by consuming the spiciest buffalo wings on the face of the earth.

"I'm dedicating this record to my best friend, Macy," EJ says to the crowd. "One time I watched her eat a whole jalapeño pepper in one bite! It made her eyes water and her nose run, but she loved it. If she can do that, I can do this!"

The wings EJ will be eating are so spicy that she has to wear plastic gloves while handling the food, or her skin could blister and break out in a rash. She's been preparing her whole life for this attempt, most recently by trying her father's spicy Sriracha sauce when he isn't looking.

"Guinness Book of World Records, *here I come!*"

EJ picks up a wing in each hand, takes a deep breath, and dives in.

Chapter 5

WHO'RE YOU CALLING CHICKEN?

Dear Diary,

Nana and Pops are driving back to Ohio today. It's been great having them here for the past week, but knowing I won't see them until at least Christmas makes me super sad. We'll still have our weekly video chats (and those are fantastic), but it's just not the same as having them here.

I think Bert can tell I'm bummed, too, because he's being an extra-good furry friend. Like last night when Nana tucked me into bed and I felt like I wanted to cry while I gave her a hug. Bert trotted into my bedroom with his favorite stuffed animal in his mouth—the green one with a long neck that looks like if a giraffe and a salamander had a baby (a galamander? or maybe a salaffe?). Bert stood next to my bed and looked up at me with a "I think you need this more than me right now" face, and he let me take the toy from him (something he never does without a fight). I love that pooch so much.

Isaac's been whiney and annoying today, which is strange, because even though he is always supremely annoying, he doesn't usually complain much. My brother has a lot of faults, but one good thing about him is that he is generally a pretty happy kid. If he's acting weird because he's sad that Nana and Pops are leaving, I can't really blame him.

EJ

EJ plodded down the steps to the living room, her feet feeling like heavy bricks. She inhaled and opened her eyes wider to try not to look as sad as she felt.

As she rounded the turn in the steps, she saw Mom, Dad, Nana, and Pops standing in a tight circle in the living room. Pops was speaking quietly—almost in a whisper—and EJ could barely make out his words. Suddenly she felt like she was walking into something she probably wasn't supposed to, but instead of going back upstairs, she dropped to her hands and knees and inched her way down the last few steps to hide behind the couch to listen.

". . .We give You control, Father," Pops prayed, his voice sincere and urgent. "I pray that Tabby and David would seek Your wisdom in this situation. And we ask that You would make it clear to them what You want them to do with this opportunity. . . ."

What situation? What opportunity? EJ wondered.

". . .It's in Jesus' name we ask these things. . ."

No, Pops! Talk more about the "situation"!

"Amen."

EJ peeked around the corner of the couch, careful not to be seen. She saw Mom and Nana in a tight embrace, Nana whispering something to Mom and tears streaming down Mom's face. Pops and Dad shook hands that ended in a hug. Something didn't sit right with EJ. This wasn't just a normal tearful good-bye to send off Nana and Pops.

Mom and Nana dried their eyes and smiled at each other, hugging once again, and then the four adults made their way through the front door to the driveway where the Winnebago sat, starting to say their good-byes.

EJ waited until they were out the door and their backs were

turned before she stood from her hiding spot.

"EJ! Isaac! Nana and Pops are leaving! Come say good-bye!" Dad called.

"Coming!" EJ said, a little too brightly, still trying not to look as sad—or now as curious—as she felt. EJ went outside and rushed to Nana, wrapping her arms around her grandmother's waist in a tight squeeze. "Can't you stay another day?"

"I wish we could, sweetie," Nana said, hugging EJ and giving her a kiss on the head. "But I can't wait for our next video chat. Are we on for Wednesday?"

"Absolutely," EJ said.

EJ reluctantly let go of Nana's waist, turned, and jumped up into Pops's outstretched arms.

"Whoa there, easy on the old man!" Pops laughed. He held her in midair then hugged her tight. "You are a gem, you know that, DG?"

"You're a gem, too, Pops," EJ said, kissing him on the cheek. "A seventy-two-karat diamond."

"Too expensive for my blood—I'm no Richard Rich." Pops smiled and set EJ back on the ground. "Now where's that grandson of ours?"

Isaac stood inside the front door, pressing his nose against the screen so it looked like a pig snout.

"Buddy, come out here to say good-bye," Mom said, motioning for him to come.

"No," he said sullenly.

"You heard your mom," Dad said a little more sternly. "Get out here to say good-bye to Nana and Pops."

Silence.

Mom and Dad gave each other the "he's *your* son" look that EJ knew so well.

"Now, Isaac!" Dad meant business this time.

The screen door squeaked open, and Isaac emerged, walking slowly toward the them, one hand under his Batman T-shirt and one on his head, like he was going to do his "I can scratch my head and rub my belly at the same time" trick. But instead of grinning, patting, and rubbing, he was whimpering and scratching.

"What is it, Isaac? What's wrong?" Mom kneeled to get down on his level.

"My throat hurts, Marmalade," Isaac said, looking pitiful. "And I itch. . .bad."

Mom lifted up Isaac's T-shirt and found the culprit of the itchiness: red, raised bumps on his skin.

EJ took a step away from her brother. She was sure he'd contracted some terrible disease from playing in the dirt and picking up bugs and worms and other disgusting things.

"Is this what I think it is?" Mom looked up at Nana, who crouched down for a closer look. Nana put her hand on Isaac's forehead.

"Red spots and a fever. Just like when you had them as a kid." Nana nodded. "But didn't they get shots for this before they started kindergarten?"

"I do remember the doctor said the vaccine isn't effective for every kid. And mine *are* exceptional in more ways than one." Mom grinned weakly, pulling Isaac in for a hug. EJ thought her brother must've been feeling sick, because he rarely let Mom hug him like that—especially in front of other people.

"Well, buddy, it looks like you've got chicken pox," Mom said. "You'll only get it this one time, and then you don't have to ever get it again."

"The bad news is you don't *actually* get to lay eggs or sprout feathers," Dad said, acting extremely disappointed at this fact. "There's not really anything too chicken-y about chicken pox."

"Oh, bummer," Isaac said. "I would like to have talons instead of fingers to help me scratch these itches."

Mom whispered something in Isaac's ear, and EJ started thinking about what animal characteristics she would want. Definitely not talons. Maybe wings, but only the kind that would let her fly. Hummingbird wings maybe. Or an opossum tail that she could hang upside down from. Or an owl's night vision. The possibilities were endless. . . .

Suddenly, out of the corner of her eye, EJ saw something streaking toward her.

EJ ducks and puts her arms over her head as an out-of-control chicken takes a leap at her, its sharp talons outstretched and feathers flying.

"ISAAC!" she shouts at the chicken. "Dad said you wouldn't *turn into a chicken!"*

Now back on the ground, the Isaac chicken cocks its head, zeroing a beady black eye in on EJ like it wants to take another go at her in an insane game of poultry tag.

"Baaach, baach, baach!" the fowl responds, a crazed look in its eye. Extending its wings in a flightless flap, the Isaac chicken runs at EJ. She doesn't know whether to try to fight it off or flee, so she just freezes and ends up in a feathery chicken embrace, Isaac's wings pinning EJ's arms down to her sides.

EJ snaps out of her daydream and realizes her chicken-poxed brother is actually hugging her. "Ew, no!" she shouts as she pries Isaac's arms open so she can get away from him. "What are you *doing*, you little creep? You're going to give me chicken pox!"

"Mom told me to!" Isaac pointed at Mom and used his other hand to scratch his shoulder through his T-shirt.

EJ looked at Mom, who was trying to hide a smile behind her hand. Dad, Nana, and Pops just outright grinned at her.

"What gives?" EJ put her hands on her hips and glared at Mom. "You *want* him to *infect* me?"

"Actually, I do," Mom said. "EJ, you haven't had chicken pox yet, and if the vaccine doesn't work on Payne genes, the sooner you get sick, the better."

"Why?" EJ demanded.

"You're going to church camp in a few short weeks," Dad said. "So the sooner you get chicken pox, the sooner you can get over them."

Camp. The thought that Isaac's chicken pox plague could keep her from going to Camp Christian gave her the resolve she needed. EJ swallowed to check if she had even a hint of a sore throat yet.

Nothing.

An idea—perhaps the most disgusting idea EJ had ever had in her life—suddenly popped into her brain.

"Hey, Isaac, you know what would be good for your sore throat?" EJ asked.

"What?"

"A cherry popsicle," EJ said, shuddering at what she was about to suggest. "How about we go get one and share it?"

"Share it, like Isaac takes a lick and then you take a lick?" Dad asked, obviously shocked that EJ would think of such a thing.

"Uh, yeah." EJ's stomach lurched, and she wondered if she'd actually be able to go through with it. "I'm not letting chicken pox get in the way of camp!"

The shared popsicle seemed to do the trick, because forty-eight hours later a tickle started in EJ's throat. And in three days, chicken pox had arrived in full force—fever, itchy red bumps, and all. Chicken pox was downright miserable. Not only did EJ feel sick, but she was constantly uncomfortable and wanted to scratch every inch of her skin. Even the cream Mom put on the bumps to help soothe the itchiness didn't take the feeling completely away.

Since Isaac was a few days ahead of EJ in the chicken pox cycle, he started to feel better sooner than she did. The first day he was out of bed, he sneaked into her room uninvited.

Isaac: *[poking EJ in the arm]* Hey, EJ. How many chicken pox do you have?

EJ: *[waking up from dozing]* Isaac, get out. I'm sleeping.

Isaac: No, you're talking. You can't be asleep if you're talking.

EJ: *[closing her eyes and rolling over]* I'm a superhero, and talking in my sleep is one of my super strengths. Get out.

Isaac: I counted 106 chicken pox on me. Mom had to count my back.

EJ: I don't care.

Isaac: Do you want me to count your back, EJ?

EJ: It's not a contest, Isaac.

Isaac: But it *could* be.

EJ: *[silence]*

Isaac: One. . .two. . .three. . .four. . .

EJ: ISAAC! OUT! NOW!

Chapter 6
THE SWING SET SWITCHAROO

Dear Diary,

Dad built a swing set in the backyard the spring after I was born. A swing, a baby swing, a trapeze bar, monkey bars, and a clubhouse with a slide. Over the years, Isaac and I have spent so many hours out there—when we wanted to play outside and when Mom and Dad made us play outside because we were driving them nuts— and I have a ton of fun memories from those times. But the truth is, the swing set is too small for us now. (In other words, it's lamesauce.)

So Dad came up with a great idea for a project he's calling "The Swing Set Switcharoo." All winter Dad, Isaac, and I worked on plans for how we were going to take the individual pieces of the swing set and create something brand-new: a tree house in the huge oak tree in the backyard. I'm talking a sweet rope ladder, fireman's pole, front door, curtains in the windows—all with a bird's-eye view of the entire neighborhood. Dad says every kid needs a home away from home, and there's nothing wrong with making it totally cool! (Seriously, my dad is the best.)

We've been working on it together a few hours every weekend since school let out, and today is the day we'll finally get it done. Just a few finishing touches, and we can call it home-sweet-tree-house!

EJ

P.S. Two weeks and two days till C-A-M-P!

"EJ, would you take these out with you?" Dad handed EJ a box of three-inch screws he pulled from a drawer from his garage workbench.

"You got it." EJ wedged the box into the tool belt around her waist. "You need anything else to go, Dad?"

"That's it for now," Dad said, picking up his own tool belt and slinging it over his shoulder. "I'll join you out back in just a second."

EJ walked toward the side door of the garage that led to the backyard and whistled for Bert to follow her. The two strolled through the door into the sunshine of the warm summer day.

EJ paused halfway through the yard to inspect their work so far. The tree house was about ten feet off the ground, with a rope ladder that led from the ground up to a trap door on the front porch of the tree house. The porch had a railing on all sides except the back, where there was a fireman's pole anchored to the tree house roof—for quick escapes. The tree house itself was a one-room square building big enough for four people, and the roof was high enough that Dad could stand up inside without ducking. A door led inside from the front porch, and there were window openings on the other three walls. EJ's favorite part of the house had been Dad's awesome idea—a "sky hatch"—a swinging door in the roof that opened with a pulley system so they could watch the clouds by day or stargaze by night. He had gotten the idea from an old movie called *Swiss Family Robinson*, where a family was shipwrecked on a deserted island and had to build their own shelters to survive.

It was almost hard for EJ to believe that the tree house was made entirely from their old swing set. In fact, the only evidence left that there ever was a swing set at all was the lone baby swing, lying on its side next to the trunk of the tree.

"EJ! I'm putting up my dinosaur posters on the walls." Isaac poked his head out of the window and waved his toy hammer at her. "You'd better come and stop me!"

"You know what Mom said!" EJ yelled up at him. "No decorating until we decide on a name!"

"Yeah, I know." Isaac grinned down at her with his missing-tooth smile. "I just wanted to see what you'd say."

"Brothers." EJ rolled her eyes.

EJ walked to the five-gallon bucket that was sitting on the ground at the base of the tree, set the box of screws inside, and tugged on the rope that attached the bucket to the tree house above. "Special delivery, Isaac!"

"Oooh, yes!" Isaac pulled on the rope, and the bucket slowly rose off the ground. "I hope it's the dinosaur-scented air freshener I ordered!"

"Even better than that," EJ called up. "A box of screws!"

"You two ready to get started?" Dad called as he walked across the yard, his arms full of lumber. "All that's left to do is get these shutters assembled and installed, and we can call this Swing Set Switcharoo finished. . .aroo!"

"Dad, what do you want me to do with this baby swing?" EJ poked at the plastic swing with the handle of her hammer. "Want me to go put it on the thrift store donation pile?"

"No, I think I'll hang it from that limb over there." Dad pointed to a sturdy-looking branch on the oak tree.

"But why—" EJ didn't get her question out before Mom called, "I've got surprises for everyone!" She walked across the yard, dragging a couple of big shopping bags behind her.

Dad's face lit up when he saw Mom. "Isaac, come down for a minute. Let's see what Mom made for the tree house!"

"Be there in a second!" Isaac ran through the tree house's door and flung himself down the fireman's pole before sprinting to Mom, Dad, and EJ.

"I think that was even *less* than a second!" he panted. "A new record!"

"Eaaasy, buddy," Dad said, putting Isaac in a headlock and rubbing his head with his knuckles. "You need to keep the crazy to a minimum when you're coming down that pole."

"You guys ready to see what I have for the tree house?" Mom's eyes were bright with excitement. "I've been working pretty hard, so I hope you like them."

"Show us!" EJ said, grinning.

"Marmalade, what is it?" Isaac said, pulling himself out of Dad's headlock and stepping toward Mom to try to look in a bag.

"First, something to add a little homeyness to your new place." Mom revealed a set of window curtains—with cartoon dinosaurs on them. "What do you think?"

"Excellent!" Isaac's eyes widened. "Those will go great in the Dino Den!"

"Those are really. . .nice, Mom." EJ tried to sound happy about dinosaur curtains but was failing miserably.

"Oh, really?" Mom said, sounding skeptical. "I thought you might like *these* better." With a quick tug on the fabric, Mom pulled the curtains inside out to reveal red fabric with gold and silver stars that shimmered in the sunlight—not a single dinosaur in sight!

"Oh man!" This time it was EJ who was amazed. "Mom! Those

are *cool*! How did you do that?"

"I'll show you how to switch curtains once I install these bad boys," Mom said. "And since you couldn't come up with a name that would work for both of you, why not have two names?"

Mom held up a wooden nameplate on a string that she had painted herself. One side said Isaac's Dino Den and the other side said EJ's Star Palace.

"You can hang it on the nail that's next to the front door," Mom explained. "And I have one more surprise. . . ." Mom pulled back the big plastic bags to reveal what was inside: two oversized beanbag chairs, one covered in Isaac's dinosaur material and the other in EJ's red-with-stars material. "Homeyness plus comfyness! What do you think?"

"I think we may never see our kids in our own house anymore," Dad said as EJ and Isaac plopped down into their new chairs with big smiles on their faces. "On second thought, this tree house is going to be so rad that maybe *I* want to move out here, too!"

EJ laughed. "No, Dad! Kids only." Then she added, "Well, adults can come—but by invitation only."

Dad had a far-off look in his eye, still imagining living in the tree house. "I'd call it the Dad Cave. Yeah, that has a nice ring to it."

"That paint job on the shutters looks great, David," Foreman EJ says as she observes one of her best employees. "Think we'll be ready to hang them on time?"

"Yes ma'am," David says, raising his paintbrush to his forehead in a salute, leaving a smudge of green paint on his hard hat. "Right on schedule."

EJ nods and encourages David to keep up the hard work. This is the biggest, most important house construction she's ever overseen, and so far everything has gone according to plan. The only strange thing is that nobody knows who is actually going to live in the house. The whole job was commissioned anonymously, but since the payments keep coming, EJ has found no reason to complain or even question who is behind it.

Ten thousand square feet of living space, complete with a bowling alley and driving range in the lower level, a forty-seat state-of-the-art movie theater (with plush reclining seats), an Olympic-size swimming pool in the backyard with eight waterslides emptying from the house's second floor into the pool, a full arcade with video games and skee-ball (EJ's favorite), eleven bedrooms, and fifteen bathrooms—EJ wouldn't mind living in this house once it's all done.

EJ walks into the living room to check on the interior decorator named Tabby, who is installing curtain rods and curtains.

"Looks amazing," EJ says, admiring her work. "Do you know who is supposed to be moving into this place when it's done?"

"All I've heard is that it's some kind of famous inventor," Tabby says, adjusting the curtains so they hang evenly across the window. "Whoever it is must be extremely rich, so I'll be interested to hear what he invented."

A young boy walks into the room, sipping from the juice box in his hand and dragging a beanbag chair behind him. "Hi!" he says between sips. "Is the arcade ready yet?"

"Excuse me, but this is an active worksite," EJ says, making sure that her "foreman" name tag on her chest is visible. "You need to have a hard hat on. And by the way, who are you?"

"I'm the owner," he says. "This is my house."

"Wait a second," EJ says, *not believing him even a little bit.*
"What did you invent that made enough money to build this house?"

The boy holds up his juice box and pulls the straw out. "Bendy
straws," he says. "Just think about how much better they make our
lives. Kids love 'em. Adults love 'em. There's all kinds of money to be
made in bendy straws."

"Oh Isaac, I never know what you're going to come up with
when someone asks you a question." Mom laughed as she used a
power screwdriver to finish putting up the last curtain rod.

"My genius brain surprises me sometimes," Isaac said, sitting in
his beanbag chair and slurping the remaining juice.

A few minutes later, EJ and Dad were hanging shutters—EJ in
the tree house, with her head and arms sticking out the window,
Dad standing on a plank of wood that was lying across the rungs
of two stepladders. They were halfway done when Dad's cell phone
rang in his pocket.

"Hi, Steve!" Dad held the phone to his ear with his right
shoulder while he checked to make sure the shutter was level.
"Right now? Yes, I know it's hard to get everyone together. Sure,
that's no problem. Give me ten minutes and I'll be there."

EJ's heart sank. As a pastor, Dad sometimes got phone calls
at home that meant he had to leave quickly—an accident or a
sudden sickness of someone in the church and he'd need to rush
to the hospital. Sometimes he could just be a calming person in a
situation, and he loved people so much that he was happy to do
it; he said it was part of his calling. And EJ loved that Dad loved
people so much. But that didn't make it any easier when he had to
leave in the middle of something fun like finishing the tree house.

"Hey, hon?" Dad called up to Mom, who was painting the

railing on the front porch with Isaac. "The guys on the church board want to meet to talk about some stuff. . .about the thing. Shouldn't be long."

Stuff. . .about the thing? EJ's mind immediately went back to the teary prayer circle between Mom, Dad, Nana, and Pops. All this secretive talk reminded EJ of when she was four and her parents would spell things in front of her so she didn't know what they were *actually* talking about, which would sometimes result in confusing conversations:

Dad: Tab, I'm thinking we should get some I-C-E C-R-E-A-M tonight.
Mom: But I have C-O-O-K-I-E-S for tonight, dear.
Four-year-old EJ: No! I don't want to take a nap!

"Dad, why are you meeting with the church board?" EJ asked, trying to sound casual. "Aren't your normal meetings the first Tuesday of the month?"

"Nothing you need to worry about, EJ," Dad said, hopping off the makeshift scaffolding to the ground. "Adult stuff. Boring."

Dad's answer didn't satisfy EJ's curiosity. If anything, it made her wonder even more.

"Be back in a jiffy, and we'll fire up the grill for hamburgers for supper."

"We'll finish up that last set of shutters," Mom said. "EJ, can you show me the ropes once I finish this coat of paint?"

"Yeah," EJ said absentmindedly as she watched Dad walk to the garage. She made a mental note similar to the ones she made in her notebook as EJ Holmes:

1. Mom crying
2. Unscheduled meeting with church board: stuff. . .about the thing.

What was going on?

Chapter 7

The Bad ~~Winner~~ Loser

Dear Diary,

Macy and her mom are coming to our house this morning. Our moms have started clipping coupons together, and they seem to think it'll be good mother-daughter time if Mace and I help them. Cutting and organizing coupons sounds like the number one most boring thing I could possibly be forced to do. But I figure once Macy and I help for a while, they'll let us go play outside, and I can show her the tree house!

Tonight after supper we have a family game night planned, with all of our favorites: Chickenfoot (a game played with dominoes where the pieces are arranged in a way that looks like a bird's talons), Uno (the best card game there is), and Mouse Trap (a crazy board game that ends up with a chain reaction in which you try to capture other players' mice in a cage).

And I'm pretty much the best at all of them.

Here's something you should know about me, Diary: I love playing games. Well, actually, I like ~~winning~~ DOMINATING games. Mom and Dad are always trying to get me to be a better winner, and I tell them I'm a great winner—I win all the time! But I guess that's not what they mean by "better winner."

The truth is, Diary, it feels so good to rub the loser's (Isaac's) nose in his loss! Anyway, aren't adults always saying that losing builds character or something like that?

EJ

EJ stuck out her tongue while she concentrated on cutting out a fifty-cent-off coupon for dish soap.

"EJ, you don't have to worry about the edges being perfectly straight," Mom said as she filed a coupon in her binder.

"I'm trying to make my coupons as perfect as Macy's," EJ said, breaking her concentration when the paper caught in the scissors, ripping the coupon in half. "Oh rats."

Perfectly cut coupons were just the beginning of the differences between EJ and her best friend. EJ wished she knew Macy's secret to looking and acting so cool, calm, and collected. Macy's shoes were always tied (EJ usually tripped over her shoelaces), Macy's coffee-colored hair always lay perfectly in its adorable bob (EJ's unruly not-quite-straight-but-not-quite-curly hair had a mind of its own).

"I just try to take my time," Macy said. "It doesn't have to be perfect, though."

Macy laid a precisely cut paper rectangle on her stack of coupons on the Paynes' kitchen table. EJ looked at the hot mess of paper in front of her and wrinkled her nose.

"Will these still work even though they aren't cut straight, Mrs. Russell?" EJ asked Macy's mom.

"As long as we can still see the complete scanner code, they'll work just fine." Mrs. Russell picked up the two halves of the ripped dish soap coupon in front of EJ. "This one just needs a little tape and it'll be good as new—there!" She added the mended coupon to EJ's pile.

"You girls have been a big help cutting out the coupons," Mom said. "Thank you."

"We're done?" EJ looked at Mom expectantly. "Does that mean we can go outside and play?"

"You may," Mom said. "I'll call you in when lunch is ready in a bit."

"Have fun in the new tree house, girls!" Mrs. Russell called as EJ and Macy made a beeline for the backyard.

"That cloud looks like a snail—see its shell?" Macy pointed to the fluffy cloud through the tree house's open sky hatch. The girls were lying on their backs in the beanbag chairs, looking for interesting clouds.

"Good one!" EJ said. She pointed to a smaller dark cloud to the right of the snail. "I see a hummingbird there."

"This tree house is so great, EJ," Macy said, sitting up and looking around the room. "I think I could live here."

"So, Miss Russell, what will it take to get you into this house today?" Realtor EJ smiles at her potential home buyer—a young gymnast and Olympic gold-medal winner looking for her very first home away from her parents' house.

"Well, I'm not sure I need quite so much living space," Macy says, looking uncertain. "It's just me who will be living here. But I do really like this skylight that's in the bedroom."

"Perfect for stargazing," EJ says. "Let's go take a peek at the gym. Surely that's a must-have for every athlete."

The two walk downstairs to the fully furnished gym—uneven bars, pommel horse, balance beam, tumbling floor, and trampoline.

EJ sees Macy's face brighten and the wheels turning in her brain.

"If this was my house, I could give lessons to boys and girls who might not have enough money to pay for lessons," she says, already imagining a dozen little kids practicing their tumbling on the padded

floor. Macy thrusts her hand toward the Realtor. "I'll take it."

"I would be awesome at selling houses," EJ said, mentally adding Realtor to her list of possible career options.

A rumble of thunder sounded in the distance, and a few moments later EJ felt a sprinkle on the top of her head. She reached up to tug on the rope that pulled the sky hatch closed.

Macy stood up and looked out the window as big raindrops fell from the sky. "If I had a tree house just like this, then maybe I could move there instead of Milwaukee," she said.

"Oh yeah! Living in this tree house would be aweso— Wait. What?" EJ said, sitting up, hoping she had misunderstood what Macy said. "Did you say *move* to *Milwaukee*?"

"Yes. We might be moving there." Macy didn't make eye contact with EJ but instead fidgeted with the star curtains. "I found out last week."

"How'd you find out?" EJ asked, still soaking it all in.

"Mom and Dad had been acting funny the past few weeks." Macy looked at her toes. "Dad left unexpectedly for a business trip, and when he got back it seemed like he and Mom had a secret between them—a couple of times when I walked into the kitchen and they were in the middle of a conversation, they'd start using code words for what they were talking about."

Secrets? Code words? Macy's explanation reminded EJ of the phrases she had been trying not to think about: *"Situation. . .opportunity. . ." "Some stuff. . .about the thing. . ."*

"Then last week, I caught Mom crying while she was making salad for dinner," Macy continued, "and I couldn't take it anymore—I had to ask what was going on."

Mom—crying. Things seemed awfully familiar to EJ. Suddenly a terrible thought popped into her head: *We're moving. Maybe Dad is being called to another church—a new ministry far away. That has to be it.*

"That's when she told me Dad's getting transferred to Milwaukee for work," Macy finished miserably.

"But. . .Mace, but you can't *move*!" EJ willed herself to stop thinking about her own problems and focused on her friend. "We're going to be in the same class next year!"

Macy looked at EJ, her eyes swimming in tears about to spill onto her cheeks. "I didn't want to tell you, EJ—because when I say it out loud it makes it feel even more real."

EJ's mind whirred. She wanted so desperately to change what was happening—to fix the problems. But even though she could order off of the adult menu now, the fact was that she was still just a kid, and these things had to do with adult decisions.

She suddenly felt very helpless.

"I don't want to leave my friends—but I especially don't want to leave my best friend!" Two streams of tears forged their way down Macy's face. EJ wasn't used to seeing her friend out of sorts like this. It was usually EJ who was having some kind of drama and Macy was the one with the calming words.

EJ's perfect summer was turning out to be way less than perfect. She didn't know what to do but give Macy a hug, so that's what she did.

"Don't worry, Mace." EJ tried to make her voice as encouraging as she could, even though she felt crummy, too. *I'm worried enough for the both of us,* she thought.

Sea Fleet Naval Commander EJ Payne glances at the blinking lights on the radar screen. The enemy has been particularly hard to engage in

this battle, and she's beginning to feel the pressure.

She picks up a glass of ice water, and her hand shakes a bit, causing tiny ripples to form on the surface of the water.

"Take it easy, Payne," she whispers to herself. "You've done this a hundred times before."

EJ presses the glass to her forehead and enjoys the coolness, closing her eyes for a moment.

"Where are yooooooou, Commander Payne?" an evil-sounding voice mocks EJ over the console speaker. The person behind the voice is Sea Fleet's biggest enemy—a bad guy known simply as "The Invader."

"Your move, Commander. . .unless you want me to just go ahead and destroy you now and end your misery—"

"No!" EJ shouts back. "Just give me a second to think."

"Tick-tock," the voice sneers.

EJ rubs her eyes with her fists and tries to focus on the screen in front of her. The Invader has already destroyed four of her ships. One more hit to the final ship—the aircraft carrier that she is currently aboard—and the battle will be lost.

EJ takes a deep breath and says "E-nine," her voice sounding more confident than she actually feels.

Silence.

Hope spreads across EJ's chest—but just for a second.

"Miss!" The Invader's laugh cackles through the speaker. "Miss! Miss! Not even close!"

"Big ol' stinky miss!" Isaac pumped his fist and jumped up from his spot on the living room floor before shouting triumphantly, "B-six!"

EJ scowled and crossed her arms over her chest. There were few things in this world she hated more than losing, but losing to Isaac was *the worst.*

"You have to say it," Isaac said, grinning a toothless grin and pointing a finger at her. "Or it doesn't count."

"Then it won't count." EJ shrugged and sat back against the couch pillows. "I don't care."

"Moooom!" Isaac bellowed toward the kitchen, waking up Bert, who was snoozing in the recliner.

"All right, all right." EJ sighed and added a final red peg to her Battleship board. "Hit. Aircraft carrier sunk." Then she added quietly, "You win."

"What was that?" Isaac cupped a hand around his ear. "Who wins?"

"YOU win, but you're still a massive loser!" EJ wrenched the tiny plastic pegs and battleships out of the game board and threw them into the box. "You win. I lose. Happy?"

"Very happy." Isaac put the box lid on the Battleship game, pressing it down with both hands so it made a rude noise that sounded like expelled gas.

"Pardon me." Isaac pinched his nose and pretended to look embarrassed.

EJ rolled her eyes and tried to look disapproving at her brother, but her lips quivered into a grin, and a laugh overtook her face.

"Isaac, you are ridiculous." EJ grabbed him and poked the super-ticklish part of his neck. "But you're not going to beat me in Battleship *and* Chickenfoot dominoes. Ready to lose?"

"Never!" Isaac laughed and squirmed until he got away, scampering to the opposite side of the coffee table.

"I'm going to set up so we can start playing when Mom and Dad are done in the kitchen." EJ opened the lid of the box and removed dominoes, setting each piece facedown one at a time.

Isaac and Bert watched EJ, both with their noses peeking over the edge of the coffee table.

"You're doing it wrong," Isaac said after watching for several moments. "You're too slow."

"You *could* help me," EJ said.

Isaac stood up, and before EJ could even get a word out, he turned the box over, scattering the remaining dominoes across the coffee table and onto the floor. Bert yipped at the clattering noise and hid behind EJ.

"Isaac! Come ON!" EJ said, exasperated. "Pick up the ones on the floor before Bert decides they look like dog treats."

"Say the magic word. . . ." Isaac wagged his finger at EJ.

EJ knew this was one of those moments Mom would say that Isaac was just trying to get under her skin for the fun of it. Why? Because that's what brothers do.

"Do it before I knock you into next week!" EJ replied, a little louder than she meant to.

"Nobody's knocking anybody anywhere," Dad said as he walked into the living room, kneeled next to the coffee table, and began to pick up dominoes. "Unless it's a knock-knock joke."

"Knock-knock!" Isaac said.

"Yes, we all *Noah* good joke," EJ said. "Shut it!"

"Okay, okay, enough you two," Mom said. She was holding a tray with a big bowl of popcorn, napkins, and four plastic cups filled with fizzing root beer. "Dad and I have good news and bad news."

EJ's stomach did a nervous flip at the words *bad news*.

"The good news is that two of your favorite people are coming over to play games tonight," Dad said, reaching under the table to pick up the last stray domino.

"Did we hear our names?" As if on cue, Mrs. Winkle appeared from the kitchen, dressed in a pea-green jumpsuit with a wide purple belt and a tiny purple top hat with white feathers sticking up on the right side. EJ had always admired Mrs. Winkle's unusual fashion sense. Mr. Johnson shuffled along a few steps behind, looking pretty boring by comparison in his white polo shirt and khaki pants.

"I heard we're playing Chickenfoot tonight, so I wore my best chicken hat," Mrs. Winkle said, removing her hat to reveal an egg underneath. "My good luck charm."

"Mrs. Winkle! I have a spot right here for you." EJ patted the couch cushion next to her.

"Thank you, m'dear!" Mrs. Winkle sat and helped EJ turn the last couple of dominoes facedown.

"I didn't wear a chicken outfit, but I did bring these." Mr. Johnson picked a pair of reading glasses out of his shirt pocket and swapped them with his regular glasses. "These will make sure I can see the tiny dots on the dominoes so I can beat all of you."

"We'll see about that, Mr. Johnson." EJ gave him her best game face.

"And the bad news," Dad said, "is that Mom and I have to go to a meeting, so we're going to miss out on game night."

Again? EJ's brain yelled at her. *What is going on?*

"What meeting?" EJ asked, trying to sound casual, even though the flip in her belly had turned into a fireball in the pit of her stomach. She really hoped she'd get an actual answer this time.

"It's just something that came up last minute," Mom said as she set the popcorn and root beers on the coffee table. "But we are so thankful that Mrs. Winkle and Mr. Johnson were available to come over tonight. You all will have a great time."

EJ opened her mouth to ask another question, but Dad cut her off.

"See you in a couple hours." Dad waved as he and Mom walked out the front door. "Have fun!"

EJ snatched a cup of root beer from the tray and took a huge gulp, thinking it might extinguish the fire in her belly. The combination of the giant gulp and the fizziness of the liquid made her cough and sputter, spilling soda down the front of her green Regional Spelling Bee T-shirt.

"Oh EJ!" Mrs. Winkle quickly took the cup from EJ with one hand (to prevent any further spillage) and gently patted her on the back while EJ coughed.

"Sometimes it just goes down the wrong pipe. . . . Keep coughing," Mrs. Winkle said.

"It wasn't me that spilled this time!" Isaac said gleefully. "I call that progress!"

EJ's coughing finally calmed enough that she could grab a handful of napkins from the tray and mop up the root beer from her front. "Ugh. What a mess," she muttered, feeling the hot ball of frustration grow as the sugar from the soda made the T-shirt stick to her chest.

"No harm done, EJ," Mr. Johnson said, tossing a couple of popcorn kernels in his mouth. "No use crying over spilled. . .root beer."

"Well, are we ready to play?" Mrs. Winkle asked as she passed out the remaining cups of root beer.

"Let's get ready to ruuumble!" Isaac shouted as he picked up seven domino tiles and set them up in front of him. Mrs. Winkle,

Mr. Johnson, and EJ did the same.

EJ scanned her tiles, looking for the double nine tile to start out the game. If she was lucky enough to get the double nine, she was sure she would win.

"I've got the double nine." Mrs. Winkle smiled and set the tile down in the middle of the table.

EJ looked at her tiles again. No nines at all. She took a domino from the draw pile. Still no nine.

"Pass," she said.

Mr. Johnson looked at his tiles through his reading glasses that were propped on the end of his nose. EJ didn't wear reading glasses, but she guessed that the closer Mr. Johnson could get his glasses to the dominoes, the better he could see them. Mr. Johnson played one of his dominoes on the double nine.

Isaac and Mrs. Winkle both played nines, but that left three more nines they had to fill before open play. It was EJ's turn again, and she was still staring at a hand that didn't have any nines.

She begrudgingly picked up another domino from the pile. A double two.

"Pass," she said, tapping the domino on the table impatiently.

Mr. Johnson, Isaac, and Mrs. Winkle made quick work of filling the remaining three spots with nines. Now the board was open for EJ to play anywhere she wanted. She glanced back and forth between the table and her dominoes, searching for the very best play she could make. Then she looked for *any* play she could make. She felt the heat in her belly start to spread to her chest.

"Are you kidding me?" she said to no one. "I can't play!"

"Oh dear, I'm sure you can," Mrs. Winkle said, scooting toward her on the couch. "Want me to help you look?"

"No! I can do it!" EJ spat out the words before she could stop them, but then she saw the hurt look on her neighbor's face. "I mean—no thanks, Mrs. Winkle."

EJ looked once more at each playable spot on the table, and sure enough, none of her dominoes matched. She drew a tile from the pile and barely looked at it, sure it would be another dud.

"Pass—wait! No, not pass!" EJ double-checked the table. "I can play!" She plopped it down end-to-end with the first tile Mr. Johnson played, matching sixes. She breathed a sigh of relief and relaxed a little bit.

"Well done, EJ!" Mrs. Winkle smiled. "Remember—it's just a game."

"Heh," Mr. Johnson grunted. "A game I'm winning!" He set down a double seven domino, crossways, starting a chicken foot play. That meant the next three plays had to be sevens, to create a formation that looked like a bird's talon.

"Cock-a-doodle-doooo!" Mr. Johnson crowed triumphantly. It seemed very out of character for the former neighborhood grump. Any other time, EJ would've found it funny. Tonight it was just annoying.

"Two can play that game, Mr. J." Isaac played a seven, adding the first talon to the chicken foot. "Cock-a-doodle-doooo!" Isaac stood up and bent at the waist, pecking at the popcorn in the bowl like a chicken pecking at its feed.

"Oh, you are two birds of a feather." Mrs. Winkle chuckled as she laid a second seven on the chicken foot. Then she tucked her hands under her arms and flapped them like a hen and added, "Baach, baach."

EJ was convinced everyone had gone insane. This was a game

that would have only one winner! This was no time for fun! No room for goofiness!

The other three laughed and continued to make chicken noises, but EJ just got quiet. There were no sevens in her hand. She was going to have to draw a domino—again. She felt the heat spread from her chest up to her neck, ears, and finally her cheeks.

Maybe it was the fact that Macy was moving to Milwaukee or maybe it was because now *she* might be moving away or maybe it was because she lost a game of Battleship to Isaac or maybe—just maybe—she still wasn't 100 percent recovered from chicken pox and not quite herself (in reality, it was probably all of these things put together), but at that moment EJ simply couldn't contain the frustration she felt from her head to her toes.

In one fluid motion, EJ flips the coffee table over, flinging dominoes, popcorn, and root beer across the room. The other three stare at her in openmouthed shock.

"I can't take it anymore!" EJ shouts. "This day is the worst!"

"EJ, honey, it's your turn," Mrs. Winkle said, bringing EJ back to reality.

EJ saw that the chaos she had just imagined hadn't actually happened. She looked down at her hand to see the domino that she had just drawn. Double threes. That did it. She clenched her fist around the tile before dropping it on the table.

"Mrs. Winkle, you're going to send me to my room in about ten seconds," she said.

"You don't want to play anymore?" Mrs. Winkle looked confused.

Instead of answering, EJ picked up the bowl of popcorn, took a deep breath, and shouted as loud as she could, "I HATE THIS GAME!" Then, without warning, she turned the popcorn bowl upside down on Isaac's head. White kernels cascaded down as the bowl teetered on his head like an oversized hat.

Mrs. Winkle gasped and let out a little wail.

Mr. Johnson tried to cover up a chuckle with a fake cough.

Isaac lifted the bowl a bit and looked at EJ, eyes wide with surprise, awe, and a hint of a smile.

"Emma Jean Payne! You most certainly do need to go to your room! I've never known such a bad loser in all my life. It's just a *game*, dear."

"I know, but I like to win." EJ crossed her arms and stomped toward the stairs. "And I really needed a win today."

EJ glanced over her shoulder one last time to see Isaac, still with the bowl on his head, stuffing a handful of popcorn in his mouth. Bert sniffed the piles of white stuff on the floor.

"You know, I think this popcorn is even better now," he said, breaking the tension in the room in the way only Isaac could. "Isaac-flavored popcorn. Delicious!"

"Hey, kiddo." Dad peeked his head through EJ's bedroom door later that night. "May I come in?"

EJ nodded, put a bookmark in *The Voyage of the Dawn Treader,* and set it next to her on the bed.

"Holy moley, your room is a disaster area, EJ." A pair of jeans and a copy of *Anne of Avonlea* got caught under the door as he tried to open it. "You really need to clean up in here."

"How was your meeting?" EJ asked, hoping Dad would give a clue about where he and Mom had been.

"You and I both know I'm not here to chat," Dad said as he

shoved a wad of clothes aside and sat on the foot of her bed. "Mrs. Winkle told me what happened. But what I want to know is, why?"

EJ thought for a moment. Should she ask about the mysterious crying and secret code words and unexpected meetings? The fact was that if they were going to move, she kind of didn't want to know. At least not yet. So she decided on another approach.

"Macy might move to Milwaukee," EJ said, watching Dad's reaction.

"Macy might move to Milwaukee," EJ said, watching Dad's reaction.

"I see," he said, nodding.

"What am I going to do if I lose my best friend, Dad?" EJ felt tears stinging her eyes. He put an arm around her shoulder and pulled her next to him.

"You know, EJ, because I'm a pastor, people expect that my answer to every question or problem is to just 'pray about it' or 'read the Bible' or 'go to church more,' " Dad said. "While those are all good, doing those things isn't what it means to live by faith. If you really, truly trust God—even in the hard times like when your best friend moves to Milwaukee—that means living without worry, knowing He has your back."

"God cares that Macy is moving away?" EJ asked. She had never thought about that before.

"He cares that you're concerned about it and it's making you yell at your friends and family and dump popcorn on your brother's head," Dad said. "But He's got the future under control. He wants you to trust Him about it."

"Easier said than done," EJ said.

"You're absolutely right." Dad chuckled. "It takes guts to have faith and fully trust God. I hope you're up for the challenge, EJ."

I hope I have enough guts, EJ thought.

"Mom said if you apologize to your brother and help clean up the popcorn, we can get a couple of rounds of Uno in before bed," Dad said. "You game?"

"Yeah, just keep the soda and popcorn away from me," EJ said, grinning. Dad smiled and walked to the door, carefully tiptoeing around piles of clothes and junk on her floor.

"Hey, Dad?"

"Yes, daughter?"

"No matter what I've said in the past, I really like living in Spooner." She tried to sound as convincing as she could. "A lot."

"Ooooookaaaaaay." Dad looked at her as if she'd gone loony. "That's good to know."

Chapter 8

Jail Break

Dear Diary,

Here's the good news: CAMP STARTS ON MONDAY!
And here's the bad news: I've been banished to my room
to clean it and pack for camp. And I'm not allowed to
come out until both of those things are
done. I would much (much) rather be
outside in the beautiful weather I see just
on the other side of my window.

At least Isaac is stuck inside cleaning
his room, too.

Although, if I'm honest, Mom's right in calling my
room a "disaster area" this time. In the summertime,
it seems extra easy to let the mess get out of control.
In fact, my room sort of looks like a book,
clothes, and shoes bomb exploded—I can't
see even one square inch of the floor or the
top of my bed right now. (It took me fifteen
minutes just to find you under a pile of dirty clothes,
Diary!) And I have no idea how a lime-green flip-flop
ended up hanging by its strap from the ceiling fan in my

room. (I think I will blame my delirious, fever-y self from when I was sick with chicken pox.)

Apparently Isaac is avoiding cleaning his room as much as I am. A few minutes ago I could hear him jumping on his bed (the squeak of the mattress springs is a dead giveaway), and now I hear Isaac trying to convince Bert to clean his room. I don't care how smart and talented that dog is, he's not gullible enough to do Isaac's work for him!

EJ

EJ looked longingly out the window and sighed. The weather was perfect for setting up the sprinkler and having a good run-through with Bert (one of his favorite summertime games). The punishment she was serving seemed too harsh for her crime.

"You are hereby sentenced to time behind bars (in your bedroom) for camp-packing procrastination and cleaning laziness," the judge (Dad) had said, pounding his gavel (the bottom of his coffee mug) on the top of the courtroom bench (the kitchen table). "Take care of your responsibilities, and you may be granted an early release and a full pardon."

EJ turned away from the window to face her mess of a room. She had to get to work if she wanted to play outside before the sun went down. She took a deep breath and started.

First she pushed all the clothes off her bed and onto the floor, bulldozer style. Next she quickly made her bed—the sheets were a little rumpled under the bedspread, but it was good enough for her. Then she pulled her red polka-dot roller suitcase from under her bed, unzipped it, and put it on top.

EJ rummaged through her top desk drawer until she found a crumpled piece of paper with Mom's handwriting on it—a list of things to pack for camp. She smoothed it out by running it over the edge of the desktop. Then she sat down on her bed and read:

1. Eight T-shirts (You'll only be there for six days, but camp can get messy sometimes, so it's a good idea to have extra.)
2. Four pairs of shorts (Or to be safe, pack one pair for every day. Your choice.)
3. Eight pairs of socks and underwear (See #1.)
4. Converse All-Stars (As if you'd go anywhere without these!)

5. Flip-flops (To wear in the shower and to the lake for swim time.)
6. Two pairs of jeans (It'll get chilly in the evenings.)
7. Hooded sweatshirt (See #6.)
8. Pajamas
9. Bathing suit (DON'T FORGET THIS ONE!)
10. Shampoo, conditioner, soap, deodorant, toothbrush/toothpaste
11. Hairbrush and ponytail holders (If you're lucky, you'll have a dorm mom who will be able to fix your hair in French braids!)
12. Bug spray (You're so sweet, the mosquitoes will eat you up!)
13. Flashlight (It gets dark at night at camp. Also fun for flashlight tag in the dorms.)
14. Diary and pen (To record all the fantastic memories you make at camp!)

EJ smiled as she set the list on her bed. She liked how specific Mom was on the list. Scratching the remnant of a chicken pock on her elbow, EJ wondered how all this stuff was supposed to fit in her little suitcase.

"All right, EJ. You can do it." EJ gave herself a little pep talk as she dove into the mounds of stuff on her floor. Every time she found a piece of clothing on the packing list, she sniffed it to determine whether it was clean or dirty. If it was clean, she tossed it into the suitcase. If it was dirty, it went into a laundry basket. If it wasn't obvious by the sniff test whether it was clean or dirty, EJ gave it the benefit of the doubt and tossed it in the suitcase.

By the time she'd found all the clothes on the list, her room was looking quite a bit cleaner. A dozen books made their way to their spots on the bookshelf, eliminating even more clutter. Next she picked up shoes and matched them in pairs before lining them up in her closet. For a half second, she couldn't find the mate to a lime-green flip-flop, but then she remembered it was hanging from the ceiling fan, so she stood on her desk chair to get it down before slipping both sandals in the front zipper pocket of her luggage.

EJ had just started flattening the pile of clothes into her suitcase to get them to fit (folding clothes was a giant waste of time), when she heard a crunching noise coming from the small door that joined her room with Isaac's. Until a couple of years ago, this was a fun "secret passage" that she and her brother would use to sneak back and forth between their rooms while they played. Until the day it wasn't fun anymore.

EJ remembered it like it was yesterday: her ninth birthday—a slumber party with the girls from EJ's class at school. Isaac sneaked through the secret door after lights-out wearing a Darth Vader mask that changed his voice to sound like the evil villain from the Star Wars movies. He woke up EJ and all her guests by yelling, "Luke. . .I am your father!" which was followed by seven full minutes of shrieking and screaming (the girls) and barking (Bert) before Mom and EJ could get everyone calmed down.

The secret passage door had been firmly locked from EJ's side since.

Crunch, crunch.

EJ tiptoed toward the door and listened.

The crunching stopped.

She held her breath.

The crunching started again.

EJ quietly unlocked and slowly twisted the knob before

yanking the door open and shouting "Hey!" Isaac snapped his head up, eyes wide in surprise. His hands were still on the piece of paper he was trying to shove under the door, but the carpet was too high on either side for him to do it very easily, so the paper was getting more and more mangled each second his little fingers tried to get it to go under.

"What is this?" EJ snatched up the paper and saw that Isaac had written a note:

> will you play with me?
> Yes
> No
> ((ircle one)

"Isaac, I'm busy!" EJ crumpled the paper and chucked the ball so it bounced off his forehead. "And you're supposed to be cleaning your room, too!"

EJ slammed the door closed before Isaac could respond (or throw the paper wad at *her* head) and jammed the doorknob lock button till it clicked.

"But you didn't circle one," she heard Isaac say through the door.

EJ ignored him and returned to her bed, checking the list to see what she was still missing. Bug spray? She'd need to get that from Mom. Toiletries? Diary? She decided she would pack those at the last minute since she would still need to use them before she left for camp. Flashlight? She dug in her desk's bottom drawer until she found her favorite red flashlight. She flicked it on and off a couple of times to make sure it worked and then tucked it in her suitcase among the mass of wadded-up clothes. She mentally checked off items from her list: socks, underwear, T-shirts, shorts, jeans, hoodie, shoes. . .

"Oh! My swimsuit!" EJ had nearly forgotten the most important thing to pack for camp. She opened up the bottom dresser drawer and pulled out her favorite suit—a red tank with three gold stars on the front. She folded it in half and then in half again and gently laid it on top of everything else in the suitcase.

Finished packing (at least for now), EJ zipped her suitcase closed and scooted it to the end of the bed. She looked around her room and was pleasantly surprised to see that packing had pretty much taken care of the cleaning, too.

Crunch, crunch.

Inmate EJ knows that all-too-familiar sound. It's the prisoner in the next cell, Isaac, sending her a message the only way he can without the guards knowing—through a crack between their cells.

Both EJ and Isaac claim to be innocent of the crimes that landed them in the slammer. But at this point, it doesn't matter. They've been working on an escape plan for months, and after three long years behind bars, today's the day they're going to get out, and get out for good.

EJ has just been waiting for the signal.

Crunch, crunch.

A corner of the paper sneaks its way through the crack, and EJ is just able to pinch it with her fingertips to pull the note through.

Time to go.

Those three little words are the signal EJ is waiting for. She quickly removes a bobby pin from her hair and uses it to pick the lock between their cells. After a minute of work, she feels a click and the door swings open.

"We don't have much time," Isaac says, looking back into his cell before closing the door. "The warden is making rounds today, so we have to get out while the getting's good."

"How much time?" EJ asks, starting to work on the window lock. They both freeze as they hear a voice in Isaac's empty cell.

"Isaac? Isaac!" Mom's voice filtered through the door. "Come out, come out, wherever you are!"

"Isaac! The jig is up!" EJ whispers. "Hide under my bed." Isaac runs and slides under the prison cot head first.

A moment later, EJ heard a knock on her bedroom door. EJ (not-so-gently) kicked Isaac's left foot, which was still peeking out from under the bed a split second before Mom stuck her head in the door.

"Ow!" Isaac said, while EJ pretended to sneeze to cover up the sound.

"Bless you. Hey, it's looking good in here, EJ," Mom said, glancing around the room. "Are you all done packing?"

"All packed but a couple of last-minute things," EJ said, stepping in front of the bed to try to hide any Isaac body parts that might try to make an appearance.

"Fantastic. Well, you've served your sentence, and you can leave your room anytime you want to," Mom said. "Oh, and I can't find Isaac, but his room is clean, so he's free to go, too."

"Thanks, Marmalade!" Isaac called from under EJ's bed.

Mom chuckled as she left the room.

"Well, there goes our jail break," EJ said, disappointed their daydream was ruined. "We don't have to stay in our rooms anymore."

"Unless we just break out for the fun of it," Isaac said as he crawled out.

"What do you have in mind?" EJ asked.

Isaac looked out the window and pointed at the flat roof that covered the front porch. "Dare me to jump from that roof to the ground?"

"Triple-dog dare you!" EJ grinned. No way Isaac could say no to a triple.

"Here goes nothin'!" Isaac raised the window and hopped out onto the shingled roof. He turned and gave EJ a thumbs-up sign just before Bert started barking like a maniac in the yard below.

"ISAAC DAVID! What are you *doing*?" Dad bellowed from the ground. "Sit down before you fall and break your neck!"

EJ mostly disappeared below the open window but continued to peek a little bit over the windowsill. *Sorry, kid,* she thought. *You're on your own.*

"But it was a triple-dog dare, Dad!" Isaac tried to plead his case while he scooted toward the edge of the roof and let his feet dangle down.

"I don't care if it was a quadruple-dog dare. This is violating your terms of parole," Dad said as he reached up and firmly grabbed Isaac's legs before pulling him safely to the ground. "Back to the slammer for you."

Chapter 9
Off to Camp

Dear Diary,

It's finally here: the day I've been waiting for since I was a Camp Christian day camper. My week of church camp starts today!

Dad says that Camp Christian is one of those special places that a lot of the kids in Wisconsin get to experience together, so we all have similar memories that last a lifetime. I think it's pretty cool that Dad still keeps in touch with 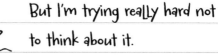 some of the friends he made at camp. A couple of his camp buddies were even groomsmen in Mom and Dad's wedding.

Macy and I are going to have so much fun this week, Diary. This will be her first time at summer camp, so I can't wait to experience this week together! I just wish this wasn't possibly our last week of camp together, too.

 But I'm trying really hard not to think about it.

Isaac is super bummed that

he's not going to a week of camp, although I'm not going to be free of him for the entire week, because one of the days he'll be there for day camp with all of the other babies. I'm just hoping to avoid him as much as possible that day. Maybe I'll try to disguise myself so he doesn't even recognize me.

Well, Diary, you're the last thing I need to pack in my bag before we load up and drive to camp, so into the suitcase you go!

EJ

"Bye, sweetie," Mom called one last farewell as she walked out of the girls' dorm room with Dad and Isaac, both of them gently tugging on an arm. "Have a fantastic week!"

"Love you!" EJ waved as her family disappeared around the corner. She was the first girl in the dorm room, and she and Mom had already made her bed, so she decided to do some unpacking.

EJ sat on her lower bunk and unzipped her suitcase. The wadded mass of clothes she'd stuffed into the luggage two days ago made the top fly open like it was spring loaded—three T-shirts, a pair of shorts, and two pairs of socks exploded onto her bed. Something else she didn't recognize flopped out onto the clothes, too—a small book that landed with a little bounce.

EJ picked up the book—a pocket-size Bible with a worn leather cover. She traced a finger over the gold lettering of the words HOLY BIBLE. Then she saw the name stamped at the bottom corner of the cover: DAVID PAYNE. She opened the front cover and found a note with her name on it.

Dear EJ,

My parents gave me this Bible for my very first week of church camp when I was ten—all the way back in 1986. (Yes, I know. I'm old.) And now that you're at your first week of camp, I want you to have it. If you look hard enough, you might find some handwritten notes in the margins that I took while I was at camp.

I know you have been looking forward to this week for a long time, EJ—and it's going to be the best week of your summer. Soak up every second of swimming, boating, tent sleeping, campfire-ing, archery-ing, and *everything else in store for you. Listen for God's voice in the fun and exciting times—and in the quiet times, too. Listen for Him and look for Him in the pages of this Book. He'll teach you what He wants you to know.*

Mom and I are proud of you, EJ. God is, too.

Love,
Dad

"That's a pretty sweet Bible."

EJ looked up and saw a smiling face of a young woman carrying a sleeping bag under her arm and pulling a roller suitcase behind her.

"Thanks!" EJ smiled. "It's my dad's. Somehow he put it in my suitcase without me knowing it."

"Doesn't look like it'd be too hard to hide a stowaway Bible in that hot mess of clothes you've got there," the girl said, pointing to the clothes explosion on her bunk. "I've got something here that might help with all those wrinkles."

She unzipped a suitcase pocket, produced a spray bottle labeled WRINKLE RELEASER, and handed it to EJ. "This stuff is a lifesaver for us college students. Who has time to iron? I'm Susan, by the way—your camp counselor and dorm mom."

EJ took the spray bottle from Susan. With her long brown hair in two braids, a green Camp Christian T-shirt, khaki shorts, green-and-white-striped knee socks, and white tennis shoes, Susan looked every bit the part of a camp counselor, EJ thought.

"I'm EJ Payne," EJ said, spraying a tentative spritz of the wrinkle releaser on a T-shirt.

"Come on, EJ, you've got to show those wrinkles who's boss or they're not going to leave." Susan picked up another wrinkled T-shirt and hung it on a hanger next to EJ's bunk. "Let me show you."

Intrigued, EJ handed Susan the spray bottle. Susan pumped several sprays onto the wrinkles and tugged on the shirt to smooth the whole thing. "There, just like that, and you'll have wrinkle-free camp clothes as soon as they air dry."

"Cool, thanks!" EJ hung up all the clothes from her suitcase and began spraying and tugging one piece at a time while Susan made up her bunk across the room.

"When will everyone else get here?" EJ asked.

Susan checked her watch. "Anytime now," she said. "Since we're the farthest dorm away from registration, dorms A through D are probably filling up first."

"I didn't mind the walk, because I wanted to stay in dorm E. You know, for my name." EJ wondered if that was a babyish reason for picking a dorm. "Plus, this is the one I told my best friend I'd be in."

"Both are good reasons for being in this dorm," Susan said, shoving her empty suitcase under her bunk. "I'm glad you're here, EJ. I can tell we're going to be friends."

Just then, CoraLee McCallister appeared in the doorway looking wild-eyed and desperate.

"Is there room in here?" she demanded. "Open bunks?"

"Hey, I'm Susan." The dorm mom stood up from her bunk and smiled. "And you are. . . ?"

"In need of a place to sleep! The other dorms are filled up already!" CoraLee snipped and then called over her shoulder, "Mom, I *told* you we left home too late to get a good spot!"

CoraLee's mom and sister, Katy, stepped into the room. Her

dad, a few steps behind, was struggling to carry two huge suitcases, hanging clothes, and bedding.

"Wow, looks like someone plans to be here all summer," Susan said, an obvious teasing tone in her voice.

"CoraLee has packed only the necessities for a comfortable week away from home." Mrs. McCallister had an edge to her voice. "We McCallister women don't do well *roughing it*."

"Oh, right. Sure." Susan didn't seem to know how to respond. "CoraLee, which bunk would you like to claim?"

CoraLee pointed to the bunk directly above EJ's. "That one will be fine," she said. Her dad moved toward the bunk and dropped everything next to it as if he couldn't carry the heavy load for another second.

"CoraLee, that one's reserved for Macy," EJ said, poking out her head at the foot of the bunk bed.

"EJ! Hi!" Katy McCallister rushed to EJ's bed and plopped down next to her. "I love your sleeping bag—red is my favorite color!"

"Thanks, Katy." EJ smiled to herself. Ever since she had realized last year that Katy wanted to be just like her (and not CoraLee), she thought maybe CoraLee was a little jealous. "Are you coming to day camp this week?"

"I don't see Macy's name on that bunk." CoraLee narrowed her eyes at EJ. "And that's the bunk I want."

"How about the one above me?" Susan offered, patting the mattress. "I promise I don't roll around at night much or snore too loudly."

"On second thought, I think I want to stay as far away as I can from this Payne-in-my"—CoraLee saw the disapproving look she was getting from her mom—"uh, I mean, I'll just take a bunk at the back of the room."

Mr. McCallister sighed and reloaded his arms with luggage and bedding and followed CoraLee and his wife to the back of the room, where CoraLee was already loudly complaining that her mattress didn't have a memory foam top.

"Yep, I'm coming to day camp," Katy said as she stood up to reluctantly follow her family. Then her face brightened. "Maybe you can be my big buddy!"

"I'd like that. I'll see what I can do," EJ said. Weeklong campers would be assigned day campers to be "big buddies/ little buddies." EJ knew it was a way to keep track of the little campers—but if she could have a cool little buddy like Katy (and not get paired up with Isaac), it might not be so bad.

"Awesome!" Katy gave EJ a big smile. "See ya later, alligator!"

"After a while, crocodile," EJ said.

EJ watched as girls and their families showed up in the doorway, all looking for empty bunks. Susan made quick work of ushering them in and getting everyone situated. EJ appreciated that Susan steered clear of the bunk she was trying to save for Macy. Soon the room was a hum of excited energy.

"EJ! I'm coming!" EJ heard Macy shout down the hallway even before she could see her. Two seconds later, Macy ran into the room, a sleeping bag tucked under one arm and a pillow under the other. "Am I late?"

"No, you're right on time, Mace!" EJ grabbed the pillow from her friend and tossed it on the top bunk. "There, now it's officially your bed."

Mrs. Russell walked into the room, Macy's big canvas

gymnastics bag on her shoulder. "Here we go, Macy," she said as she set the bag at the end of the bunk. "Good-bye, my love!" She pulled Macy in for a quick hug and kiss on her forehead.

"Aw, Mom!" Macy wiped off the kiss. "Have a good week. I love you. Tell Dad I love him, too. And tell Bryan not to touch my stuff while I'm at camp." Bryan was Macy's fifteen-year-old brother.

"Take care of Macy this week, EJ," Mrs. Russell said as she walked toward the door. "You girls have a week full of memories!"

"We will, Mrs. Russell," EJ called after her. *Our first and last time at camp,* EJ thought miserably.

In a matter of minutes, the remaining bunks in the room were claimed, and soon the last parents and siblings cleared out of the room after saying final good-byes. Sleeping bags and pillows of all colors topped each mattress, and girls were chattering and giggling and bouncing on beds while getting to know each other before camp officially started. EJ and Macy sat next to each other on Macy's top bunk, their legs dangling over the side while they read through the camp booklet that explained the week.

They oohed and aahed as they read about swimming, jet skiing, horseback riding, canoeing, bumper boats, a candy store and soda fountain called the Snack Shack, archery, and the high ropes course and zip line. EJ wondered how they'd be able to fit so much awesomeness in one short week!

Just then, the *bong-bong-bong* of a bell sounded in the distance.

"There's the bell, girls!" Susan said, checking her watch. "Head out to the hillside for the camp picture, and after that supper in the dining hall. Camp has officially started!"

"You boys in the front row—stop that tomfoolery!" the lanky, red-headed camp counselor named Gene yelled through a megaphone.

"Who is Tom Foolery, and how do we stop him?" The words coming out of Cory Liden's mouth may have sounded like he was sassing the camp counselor, but EJ was actually wondering the same thing.

Gene, dressed in an orange Camp Christian T-shirt, khaki cargo shorts, white tube socks, tennis shoes, and a floppy fisherman's hat, stood behind a camera on a tripod, glaring at the boys in the front row. The entire camp—about two hundred campers and counselors—stood on the hillside to get a group shot to commemorate the week. (Dad still had the photos from every week of church camp he attended. EJ loved looking at the faces in the crowd and making up stories about the particularly interesting-looking ones.) Gene had been trying to take the camp picture for the past ten minutes, but a group of boys in the front row—mostly boys from EJ's church—kept ruining the picture by posing ridiculously at the exact moment Gene snapped each shot. For the first picture, they turned around so their backs were toward the camera. Then they all saluted, crossed their eyes, and stuck their tongues out. After that they jumped and pumped their fists in the air. Next they played air guitars. For the last shot they picked up a camper named Michael Draper and sat him on their shoulders.

The rest of the campers, who were amused by the boys' antics at first, were quickly losing interest under the hot sun. Plus, supper in the dining hall smelled exceptionally delicious. (EJ thought that at least half of the camp could probably hear her stomach growling.)

"Gene, they're fifth graders—not senior citizens," Susan said to Gene as she walked toward him. "You've got to speak their language." Then she turned around and addressed the boys.

"Tom Foolery was a camper who didn't know when to stop messing around, and because he didn't listen to his camp counselors, he lost swimming privileges," Susan said matter-of-factly. "So if you want to swim tomorrow, boys, I suggest you learn a lesson from Tom and let Gene take this picture so we can get to dinner."

"Go, Susan," EJ whispered to Macy, grinning.

The boys looked wide-eyed at each other and appeared to silently agree to straighten up. Susan nodded at the boys and took her place in the crowd.

"Okay, everyone—one last shot," Gene called through the megaphone. "Here we go. . .ten, nine, eight—" Gene pressed the camera's timer button and ran to join the rest of the group as everyone counted down.

"Ready for the best week ever?" EJ asked Macy

"Ready!"

The girls each put an arm around the other's shoulder and grinned with the rest of the campers as the camera clicked.

"Everybody head over to the dining hall—but NO running!" Gene ordered through the megaphone. Then for added emphasis, he turned on the megaphone's siren for a few seconds. A few campers plugged their ears with their fingers and gave the gangly counselor annoyed looks. Gene didn't seem to notice.

If EJ thought Gene was a little strange, he had nothing on the crazy camp cooks, she decided. In the supper serving line, each lady was dressed up as a different US president.

"Oh yeah, I am so used to their costumes, sometimes I forget they're dressed up," Susan said, chuckling. "They'll wear different outfits at every meal."

Abraham Lincoln served grilled cheese sandwiches ("We've made four score and seven of these sandwiches, so please eat hearty, campers!"), George Washington served the green beans ("I cannot tell a lie. Green beans are my favorite vegetable."), Teddy Roosevelt served fresh fruit cups ("Bully for you!" Roosevelt said. "I'm not a bully," EJ replied, confused. "No, bully doesn't mean 'bully' to Roosevelt," the cook said. "He used that word the same way you could say 'cool' or 'awesome.' " "Oh, cool—er—bully!" EJ said, grinning.)

EJ had to ask the cook serving cookies which president she was supposed to be.

"I'm James K. Polk—this great nation's eleventh president," the cook said. "I'm probably the least-known president of all of them, so instead of quoting him, I will just tell you that you have a choice between a chocolate chip or an oatmeal raisin cookie."

"Chocolate chip, definitely!" EJ held her tray out to James K. Polk. Then she added, "Please."

"Good choice," James K. Polk said, winking.

After supper, everyone went to the rec field to play organized games—mostly a mish-mash of relay races and activities that were intended to wear out the campers so they'd go to sleep that night, despite the fact they were super excited for the week. EJ's favorite game was one they called "earth ball," which was like soccer, except with an eight-foot-tall inflated ball that reminded her of the boulder that chases Indiana Jones in *Raiders of the Lost Ark*. Instead of kicking the ball, campers would basically body slam the ball to move it down the field. The boys especially were going crazy during this game, and the camp nurse watched from the sidelines, just waiting for the first injury. EJ was sure she saw the nurse breathe a sigh of relief when they put the giant ball away and Gene announced that campfire would start in ten minutes.

The stars were just starting to twinkle in the night sky as Susan played a ukulele while she and a couple other counselors led the campers in singing silly camp songs, many with ridiculous hand motions, dances, and yelling parts. Then Susan switched instruments to an acoustic guitar and led a few praise songs. There was something extra-special about worship at camp, EJ thought. The songs were mostly the same ones they sang at church, but maybe since they were singing outside, it felt like their praises were going straight up to the heavens and not blocked by things like church roofs. EJ pushed air out of her lungs as she sang as loud as she could.

"So, you guys, our first night of camp is almost over," Susan said as she passed her guitar to another counselor. The campers all gave a disappointed groan. "But we still have the whole week ahead of us!"

Everyone cheered.

"I haven't gotten to know all of you yet," Susan said, "but one thing I *do* know is that for some of you, this week of camp might be your escape. Maybe this is a week for you to get away from a brother or sister who drives you completely crazy—"

Yep, EJ thought, smiling to herself.

"Maybe you're getting away from parents you don't get along with. Or maybe your parents don't get along with each other. Maybe this is a week away from that neighborhood kid who picks on you—or even beats you up. Or you're getting away from the pressure to be athletic enough or pretty enough or smart enough."

EJ looked around at the faces of her fellow campers and saw recognition in some of their eyes. A few even nodded their heads.

"Or maybe there's something scary going on at home. It could be anything, but it's something you don't have any control over. And you're just hoping there will be enough fun stuff at camp to distract you so you don't worry about it all week."

EJ's eyes widened, and she gaped at Susan. How did she know?

"The truth is, no matter who we are, no matter how young or old we are, we all have things in our lives that worry us and distract us," Susan said, pulling a small Bible out of her back pocket and flipping through it. "Camp is a place to hear the truth and hope God has for you. Like here, in Deuteronomy 31:8, where it says, 'The Lord himself goes before you and will be with you; he will never leave you nor forsake you. Do not be afraid; do not be discouraged.' "

The campfire cracked and popped, sending a shower of sparks up into the air as Susan made a lap around the fire ring and looked into the faces of the campers.

"Don't let his week go by without finding out what God has to say to you," she said. "His voice is always easier for me to hear at camp—as long as I'm listening."

I'm listening, EJ thought. *As long as He's not saying Macy or I have to move.*

Chapter 10

Reptile Surprise

Dear Diary,

It's Tuesday morning at camp, and all the girls in my dorm room (me included) were up and ready to go well before the wake-up bell rang at 7:30. I think we're all just so excited to start the day that we couldn't sleep anymore!

Susan didn't seem quite so thrilled with the early morning. It might've been because we just couldn't quiet down last night after lights out. (But really, who could blame us? We're at CAMP!) Between flashlight tag and whispering and laughing across bunk beds, Susan finally pulled out the big guns and threatened to take away jet ski time if we didn't be quiet and go to sleep. After that, the room was so silent that you could've heard a pin drop. . .until CoraLee started snoring a few minutes later. (That gave me the giggles so bad that I had to get up

and walk down the hallway to get a drink from the fountain to keep from waking up the whole dorm. There was NO

WAY I was going to lose jet ski time because of CoraLee.)

Note to self: Remember that CoraLee snores in case you need to use it against her someday.

There are a ton of fun things planned for today. Rumor has it that an exotic animal wrangler is bringing some animals to camp this morning, and we'll get to see them and even play with some of them. I hope they're extra exotic and dangerous so I can show everyone how I'm a natural with animals.

EJ

EJ "the Alligator Hunter" Payne slogs through the marshy shoreline, her eyes darting back and forth under the brim of her khaki-colored pith helmet, keen on spotting any reptile movement.

"Speak to me, you magnificent beauties," she whispers.

Although many people are afraid of alligators, this famous conservationist has made it her life's goal to show people that these water dwellers are simply misunderstood. "Alligators are a lot like teddy bears," EJ was quoted as saying in a magazine article. "Razor-sharp-toothed, reptilian teddy bears who just want to be loved."

EJ is distracted by a sound she can't quite place. She cocks her head and listens intently, when, out of the corner of her eye, she sees movement in the water. The Alligator Hunter takes a flying leap into the shallow. After a moment of struggle, she stands triumphantly with a small reptile stretched high over her head in a victory stance.

"EJ, sit down!" Macy's sharp whisper cut through EJ's daydream, and she felt a tug on the hem of her shorts.

Confused, EJ glanced down to see Macy staring up at her from her seat on the ground. Macy pointed, and EJ looked up to see that Chelsea, the lead animal handler from Creative Creation Interactive Animals, was still in the middle of her presentation. And there was EJ, standing with her arms outstretched over her head, in the middle of a sea of campers who had been listening attentively but were now staring at her with looks of confusion and mild amusement.

"Yay, animals," EJ said weakly as she shook her fists over her head in a pathetic cheer. She lowered her arms and quickly sat down, trying to act like she knew what she was doing.

"Animal trainer?" Macy whispered.

"Close," EJ whispered back. "Alligator hunter."

"Nice one." Macy turned her attention back to Chelsea.

"So, as you can see by the creatures we're sharing with you today, God's creation is wild and varied," Chelsea said as she wrapped up. "And God's imagination is limitless!"

The campers applauded for Chelsea and her two assistants, but EJ knew all the campers spent most of the presentation eyeballing the animal they wanted to get their hands on. In a matter of seconds, a massive stampede of bodies rushed toward the animals.

A loud crackle and squawk of feedback came from the edge of the crowd.

"Every camper who wants to hold the animals will get a chance," Gene barked through his megaphone. "Form orderly lines, please."

The campers close to Gene's megaphone took their fingers out of their ears only when they were sure he was done with his announcement. EJ wondered if Gene liked being in charge so much that he didn't even notice how everyone seemed annoyed by his overuse of the megaphone. Well, everyone but Susan. EJ saw her staring dreamily at the male counselor with the same look in her eyes that Bert got when EJ had a bacon-flavored dog treat in her hand.

"Uh, Susan?" EJ said. Susan continued to watch Gene with a goofy grin on her face as he adjusted the knobs on the megaphone.

"Susan can't hear you," Macy whispered to EJ. "The love song playing in her head is drowning out any other sounds." EJ made a disgusted face and stuck her tongue out in a silent *blech*.

Macy cleared her throat with a pointed "ahem" to try to get Susan's attention.

"What? Oh, sorry, Macy," Susan said, flustered. "Did you need something?"

"Are you in the reptile line?" Macy asked, pointing at the line that had formed near Susan.

"Ew, no!" Susan jumped away from the line as if it were a snake. "You girls are braver than me if you want to touch those things."

EJ and Macy got in line as they watched Susan make her way over to Gene, who was polishing the bell of his megaphone with the hem of his shirt. "Girl likes boy," EJ said. "Boy *loves* megaphone." Macy laughed.

EJ turned her attention to the reptile line and counted sixteen people ahead of them. There were three other lines as well, all kids waiting to hold less sinister animals. The cuddliest animals included a rabbit and a chinchilla. (*Yawn,* EJ thought.) Slightly more interesting were the hedgehog and armadillo (the hedgehog might've been the cutest thing EJ had ever seen). Next on the danger scale was the porcupine and opossum (Dad said that he never trusted opossums because of their crazy red eyes). Finally, the truly thrilling animals—the ones that almost every camper wanted to see up close and why the line was going so slowly—included an eight-foot python named Pokey and a two-foot baby alligator named Spike.

A few minutes later, it was CoraLee's turn at the front of the reptile line, and EJ saw her point at Pokey.

"No way CoraLee's going to hold that snake," EJ said so only Macy could hear. "Miss Priss McCallister is probably afraid Pokey will get his snake slime on her pretty pink skirt."

Chelsea had CoraLee turn to face the campers in line behind her. The snake handler draped the impressive snake over CoraLee's shoulders and outstretched arms. CoraLee's eyes widened as the weight of the animal settled on her shoulders. EJ thought for sure CoraLee was a second away from shrieking in disgust and ordering Chelsea to take Pokey off. But instead, the handler leaned down and whispered something in CoraLee's ear. CoraLee gave Chelsea a questioning look, and she nodded at her. CoraLee took a deep breath in through her nose and exhaled out her mouth.

Here it comes, EJ thought. *Once she has this meltdown, I can go up there and show everybody that there* are *girls tough enough to take on snakes.*

What happened next was something that EJ couldn't have guessed would happen in a quadrillion years.

With the back of her right hand, CoraLee slowly guided the head of the snake until she was face-to-face with the reptile.

"Whoa!" The boy in front of EJ sounded truly in awe. "Check out CoraLee!"

EJ rubbed her eyes with her fists, sure that she must be having a bizarre daydream. But it was real life. The crowd murmured in amazement and pressed toward CoraLee to get a better look.

Then, without warning, CoraLee glanced up from the snake-staring contest and looked directly at EJ with a little smirk that said, "Watch this, P-A-I-N." And then, without warning, she planted a kiss right on top of the python's head!

The crowd of campers gave a collective gasp of horror that quickly turned into awe before roaring in applause and excited yelling. The boys, especially, were hooting and hollering in amazement at what had just happened.

"That might have been the single coolest thing I've ever seen!" Michael Draper said to no one in particular. "CoraLee is awesome!" Then he started chanting "Cor-A-Lee! Cor-A-Lee!" and to EJ's dismay, other campers started joining in until the entire crowd was shouting her name!

EJ couldn't believe what she was seeing and hearing. Of all the campers, the last person she thought would steal the spotlight by *kissing* a snake was CoraLee. *Two can play this game*, she thought, pushing through the crowd in front of her.

"EJ, where are you going?" Macy called behind her. "We have to wait in line!"

EJ ignored her best friend and stomped up to the alligator handler, who held the reptile with two hands—one just behind the neck and the other at the tail.

"Hey there, Spike—little Spikey-kins," she cooed at the reptile, getting face-to-face with the creature the same way CoraLee had done with the snake. "May I hold you, little guy?"

The baby alligator blinked its eyes, seemingly bored with the whole situation. Spike's handler, a blond-haired teenager named Luke, eyed EJ before handing the animal over.

"Spike's stronger than he looks," Luke said over the crowd cheering on CoraLee as she let Pokey curl around her arms like reptilian bracelets. "Are you sure you can handle him?"

"No problem," EJ said confidently. "Let me at him."

Luke held the animal out to EJ, but before she could get a firm grip, Spike whipped his surprisingly strong tail and head toward EJ, shocking her so much that she screamed and tripped backward, landing hard on her backside before Luke got the flailing alligator under control and put in its cage.

"Th–that thing wants to take a bite out of me!" she gasped, suddenly grateful that the rest of the campers were still too engrossed in CoraLee's snake show to notice her embarrassing little freak out.

"Hey, easy now. He just got spooked for some reason," Luke said, suppressing a laugh. "Not everybody can be a reptile whisperer like that girl over there."

EJ glanced over to see that Pokey was now curled on top of CoraLee's head like a hat that looked something like a beehive.

"No offense, but the rabbit might be more your speed," Luke said, pointing toward the cuddly creatures end of the exhibit. "Maybe you can work up to the reptiles."

"Hamburger or cheeseburger?" the cow asked EJ while the other barnyard animals in the serving line danced and sang multiple verses of "Old MacDonald."

"Doesn't that seem a little cannibalistic?" EJ grinned at the lunch lady dressed up as a Holstein.

"*I'm* not eating the beef, *you* are," the cow answered, laughing.

"Cheeseburger, please," EJ said, holding up her cafeteria tray.

A chicken served up celery and carrot sticks, a llama gave EJ the option of a cherry or lemon Jell-O cup (she picked cherry), and a horse gave her a carton of milk and a bottle of water.

After going through the line, she looked back when she heard a good-natured argument break out in the middle of a verse.

"Llamas hum!" the cow said. "So it should be 'with a *hmmm-hmmm* here and a *hmmm-hmmm* there.'"

"No—they spit!" the chicken replied. "'With a *pthu-pthu* here and a *pthu-pthu* there.' What do you say, camper?" The chicken pointed a carrot stick at Macy, who had been standing politely quiet with her tray outstretched, waiting to be served.

"I—uh—," Macy stammered, obviously surprised to be asked her opinion. "I guess humming seems like a better choice than spitting. . .you know, around food."

"I like the way you think, girl." The chicken added a handful of vegetable sticks to Macy's tray. "You might have a future in being a camp cook!"

EJ waited for Macy, and they found a spot at a table and sat down to eat. EJ had just licked the whipped cream off her Jell-O cup when Gene started mail call.

"When I call your name, please come up and claim your mail quickly," Gene said through his megaphone. "My lovely assistant, Susan, will have your letters in hand."

"Your *lovely* assistant, eh?" a male counselor piped up from across the dining hall. Gene's face turned a *lovely* shade of red that almost matched his hair. Susan beamed at him.

Gene's megaphone crackled as he fumbled with the switch. "Don't forget—anybody who receives a package in the mail must tell a joke in front of everyone to claim said package. It's Camp Christian tradition."

Gene started calling out names, and a steady stream of campers made their way up to Susan to claim their letters. Macy got a letter from her mom that she ripped open and started reading as she walked back to their table. Her eyes were bright and she had a strange look on her face when she sat down.

"EJ, you're not going to believe this," Macy said, shaking her head as she looked at the paper in her hand.

"What's wrong?" EJ asked, her stomach clenching with nervousness.

"Actually, nothing is wrong." Macy smiled and smoothed out the paper on the table. "Mom says we're *not* moving to Milwaukee after all! The company Dad works for is going to let him telecommute and just go to Milwaukee for a couple of days every other month."

"Mace, that's great!" EJ's stomach gave a little flip. She really was happy for her best friend, but the news reminded her of her own problem. *I'm still moving away, so I'm still going to lose my best friend.*

"Time for the packages," Gene called through the megaphone. "Anna Baker, EJ Payne, and Wade Thompson—you each have one up here. So come on up when you have your joke ready to go."

"All right!" EJ pushed her worries about moving to the back of her mind and focused on the task at hand: claiming that package.

Macy looked at EJ wide-eyed. "What joke are you going to tell? I'm glad *I* didn't get a package."

"Don't worry," EJ said, taking a final swig of milk before wiping her mouth with the back of her hand. "I was born for this."

EJ stood from her seat and walked confidently toward Susan and Gene. *Which joke should I tell?* she wondered. *The one about the magic lamp? Or maybe the talking turtle? Oh well, I'll just let my instincts take over once I can read the room.*

"EJ, the return address says your package is from your aunt CJ in Chicago," Susan said, shaking the package next to her ear. "Sounds like there's some good candy in here."

"Here you go." Gene handed EJ the megaphone, which was heavier than it looked, so she had to grasp it with both hands to keep it steady. "Just push this button when you want to talk."

EJ pushed what she thought was the correct button, except an ear-splitting siren blared out of the thing. It surprised EJ so much she accidentally threw the megaphone and watched it sail— seemingly in slow-motion—in an arc toward the floor.

"Whoa, there!" Gene fisted the megaphone strap and saved his precious contraption mere centimeters from it shattering on the floor. Gene's miraculous save was impressive, and the campers gave a collective sigh—EJ wasn't sure if it was relief or disappointment. "Maybe I'll just hold it for you," Gene said. "Ready?"

EJ took a deep breath. "Ready."

Gene held the megaphone at EJ's level and pushed the button. The megaphone gave a little squeak, so everyone knew it was on. EJ looked out at the sea of faces, all watching her expectantly.

And her mind went completely blank.

Well, *almost* completely blank. There was one joke that remained. The one joke she promised herself she'd never tell because she'd heard it too many times in her life already. The joke that made her roll her eyes and was hugely annoying because *everyone* laughed at it, even though she didn't think it was funny. At all. But what other choice did she have? She really wanted whatever was in that package from Aunt CJ.

"Knock-knock," she said.

"Who's there?" the crowd asked in unison.

"Noah."

"Noah who?"

EJ gulped. She couldn't believe she was about to deliver this punch line:

"Noah good joke?"

EJ closed her eyes, sure she'd be booed back to her seat. But after a moment of silence, a loud burst of laughter exploded from Gene and rippled through the crowd. EJ opened her eyes to see laughing faces all across the cafeteria and joined in, relieved.

Isaac's lame joke saved the day. Who would've thought?

EJ wondered if maybe she should give her little brother more credit for being funny.

Nah.

Chapter 11

Invasion of the Day Campers

Dear Diary,

Mom says that one way to set yourself up for success is to make sure your outside matches what you want your inside to be like. So I'm wearing my very favorite pair of Converse All-Stars (the red ones with the glitter that's almost worn off because they're so old), a red Camp Christian T-shirt, and my oldest and comfiest pair of jean shorts.

Why am I trying to make sure my outside matches my inside? Today is the one day of camp I've been dreading: day camp. Busloads of five- and six-year-olds

(all of whom are probably "space invaders" to their older brothers and sisters) will swarm the campground like a plague of locusts with their high-pitched voices, sticky hands, runny noses, short attention spans, and spaz-tastic craziness. And us older campers have to help herd them around all day as their big buddies!

But I'm going to try my best to enjoy camp today, Diary. And if I think about it for a half second, I

remember having such a fun time at day
camp. I especially liked hanging out with the
big kids. It made me feel so grown up. So
maybe I can be the cool friend to one of these
little ankle biters.

EJ

"All day campers should stay seated until you are paired up with your camp buddy," Gene barked through his megaphone, hardly being heard above the excited yelling, chattering, squealing sound of 150 day campers sitting on the grass of the rec field.

Well, they were *supposed* to be sitting. Mostly the boys were running around or pummeling each other or wrestling on the grass. And the girls were dancing or practicing cartwheels or picking dandelion bouquets. And there was a line of day campers being herded to the restrooms by camp counselors. (EJ thought she remembered reading somewhere it's a scientific fact that kindergarteners have the world's tiniest bladders.) Isaac was in his own little world, running through clusters of day campers and flexing his muscles. This would've been weird enough, but he was also wearing two oversized green Incredible Hulk fists and shouting, "Hulk excited! Hulk go to camp!"

"Who's the crazy day camper who's Hulking out over there?" EJ heard Cory Liden ask. "Oh wait, I recognize him. That's EJ's little brother."

"You think *that's* crazy?" EJ piped up. "That's nothing."

"He looks like fun," Cory said, grinning.

EJ and her fellow fifth-grade campers stood along the edge of the rec field, overwhelmed and amused by the heightened energy of the mass of little bodies in front of them. Three loud, crackling pops came from the megaphone. EJ assumed Gene must've jacked the volume control up to eleven—as high as it would go.

"Day campers!" Gene's voice boomed louder, but everybody knew he was fighting a losing battle. Nobody under the age of six even looked at him. "Hello? Is this thing on?"

"Gene, let me take a swing at this one," Susan said. Then she winked at EJ, Macy, and the handful of other campers near them. "Join in if you know this—just a little something I learned during student teaching."

EJ looked at Macy to see if she knew what was happening, and Macy shrugged. Susan started a very distinctive rhythmic clapping pattern—one that EJ, Macy, and the other campers from Spooner Elementary recognized as the "Zip Your Trap, It's Time to Clap" rhythm that all of the teachers used to get students to sit down, be quiet, and pay attention.

EJ couldn't help but wonder how this was going to work with *so* many kids, but she quickly joined in on the clap, keeping time with Susan. Macy and several other fifth-grade campers started clapping as well, and in a matter of seconds, the eyes of the little day campers looked toward the noise. A cluster of kindergarten boys in the middle of wrestlemania heard the clapping and—as if on cue or hypnotized by the sound—stopped beating on each other, sat down, and joined in the clapping. The swell of sound grew as more people joined in, and soon even the campers and counselors who didn't know the rhythm at first caught on to the simple beat.

It took a little more than a minute before every day camper was sitting on the ground, clapping like it was the best game they'd ever played. (EJ had always thought the "Zip Your Trap, It's Time to Clap" tactic was a little sneaky trick by teachers, but this time she didn't mind a bit since it got the day campers under control.) EJ grinned at Susan, once again admiring how resourceful and cool the counselor was. Susan ended the clap with a flourish, and 150 attentive day campers were ready to get started.

The whole scene must've caught Gene off guard, because his

precious megaphone hung at his side, and he stared openmouthed at Susan, obviously impressed with her pied piper–like skills.

"Uh, Gene. . ." Susan helped guide the megaphone to his mouth. "You've got their attention."

Gene snapped out of his daze and pushed the button. "Welcome to day camp!" A chorus of excited cheers burst out of the crowd of kids and counselors.

For the next several minutes counselors moved throughout the day campers, checked lists on clipboards, and paired day campers with their fifth-grade buddies.

Macy got paired with a tiny girl named Shawna, who looked like she was about three seconds away from bursting into tears. Macy took her by the hand and glanced at EJ with a "What have I gotten myself into?" look as she led Shawna to the dining hall for breakfast.

Cory Liden got paired up with Isaac. EJ watched and listened as Cory invited Isaac to punch him in the stomach with his Hulk fists—a request that resulted in Cory doubled over in surprised pain.

"Still think he looks like fun?" EJ asked Cory, trying to hide a grin.

"Are you kidding?" he said, recovering quickly. "Little dude is awesome!"

"Hi, EJ!" Isaac waved a Hulk fist at his sister as he and Cory walked to breakfast. "Bye, EJ!"

"EJ, you're with"—the counselor named Jen glanced down at the list—"McCallister. Katy McCallister."

"YES! Yes, yes, YESSSSSSS!" Katy leaped from her spot in the grass and skipped two circles around EJ before throwing her arms around her waist in a hug. "Best day camp EVER!"

"Eeeeasy, Katy." EJ grinned and hugged Katy back. She had to admit it felt pretty nice to be adored like that.

Breakfast was pancakes, sausage, fruit cups, juice, and milk—served by circus clowns. But everyone quickly found out there were a dozen day campers who had clown phobias, so after a handful of freak-outs and meltdowns, the cooks agreed to take off their wigs and foam noses. Still, a couple of the day campers wouldn't sit with their backs toward the cooks. "I don't trust their painted-on smiles," one day camper said, and EJ secretly agreed with him.

After breakfast they all went to the gym for a camp song sing-along, followed by a short devotion given by Gene. EJ was glad he used the building's microphone and sound system rather than giving the devotion through the megaphone.

Next up, the campers could choose from a number of different activities to do: archery lessons, boating, laser tag, pottery, kids' karaoke, jet skiing, a campfire cooking class.

EJ knew the water-related stuff would be the most popular, so she convinced Katy they should do some of the other activities first. First they sang a karaoke duet of "Lean on Me" that got a standing ovation from the crowd. Then they spent some time at the archery range. EJ made sure Isaac wasn't there; nobody in their right mind would give her maniac of a brother a weapon like that—she hoped. EJ was a little surprised to find she was a decent shot with a bow and arrow, so she mentally added that to her career list (although she wasn't really sure what kind of job involved archery).

Next EJ and Katy walked to the lake, where EJ spotted Cory and Isaac strapping on lifejackets at the boat dock.

"How do you feel about bumper boats?" EJ asked Katy.

"They're my *favorite!*" Katy replied, hopping excitedly. "But I thought you wanted to stay away from Isaac today."

"I do want to stay away from him," EJ said. "But when it comes to high seas battles, it's my turn for a win."

First Mate EJ Payne takes one last look at the map coordinates before rolling up the parchment and tucking it inside her uniform pocket. The open sea is perfect, with a brisk tailwind. She's confident the merchant ship Merriweather *will deliver its cargo of coffee and tea to the American colonies ahead of schedule.*

"Deck Cadet Katy McCallister reporting for duty, sir. . .er. . .ma'am." Katy blushes at her mistake but recovers quickly in a sharp salute to her superior.

"Ah, very good, cadet." EJ paces the Merriweather's *deck and looks out on the sea's horizon, hands clasped behind her back. "You've been through your training, and you've done well."*

"Thank you, ma'am." Katy stands a little straighter.

"I'd like you to take the helm." EJ faces Katy and lays a hand on the younger sailor's shoulder. "I've taught you everything I know, and I believe you're ready for this."

Katy's eyes light up. "Yes ma'am!" She grasps the giant wooden wheel with both hands and pulls as hard and as fast as she can, rotating the wheel clockwise.

"Stop, Katy!" EJ grabbed the edge of her seat as the bumper boat spun like a top. "Not like that! We're going to get dizzy!"

Katy let go of the steering wheel, and the doughnut-shaped bumper boat slowly stopped spinning. EJ tugged on the collar of her lifejacket and took deep breaths, willing her head to stop spinning, too.

"Sorry, EJ," Katy said sheepishly. "I thought it might be good to practice—you know, to get away from—"

"Pirates!" Deck Cadet Katy shouts, pointing toward a dark ship with black sails and a Jolly Roger flag flying from the mast. Except there was something odd about the flag—it wasn't the typical skull-and-crossbones that pirates use. No, the shape of the skull was somehow wrong. EJ raised her spyglass to get a better look.

"A T-Rex skull. Oh no," EJ whispers.

"Hoist the mainstay! Scuttle the mainmast! Protect the starboard side! Swab the poop deck!" EJ shouts frantically.

"Swab the poop deck?" Katy asks. "Really?"

"Get us out of here!" EJ replies. "It's the dread pirate Weird Beard!"

Too late. The pirate ship is already within striking distance.

"Katy, go below to take inventory of the weaponry in the cargo hold," EJ orders.

"But, ma'am, we're a merchant ship," Katy says. "What are we going to do—throw loose tea and coffee beans at them and hope it gets in their eyes?"

"Just do as you're told, cadet." EJ's voice has a warning in it that makes Katy jump to action and disappear down a ladder.

"Ahoy, matey!" Weird Beard shouts from the deck of the pirate ship. The pirate is famous for his love of Tyrannosaurus Rexes—like the Jolly Roger flag with the dinosaur head. And now that he is close enough and EJ gets a good look at him, she sees that the parrot on his shoulder isn't a parrot at all, but a bird-sized T-Rex toy that he pretends is real. . .and can talk.

Weird isn't the half of it.

"Arrrgh, what do we have here?" Weird Beard says out of the side of his mouth in a high-pitched voice—obviously his best try at being a ventriloquist with the dinosaur on his shoulder. "It be a pretty little boat sailed by a pretty little girl."

"Stand down, you vile dinosaur!" EJ doesn't know why she's talking to the toy. "Weird Beard, I can see your lips moving. You're not fooling anybody."

"Oi, don't listen to her, Cap'n," says Weird Beard's first mate, a cute pirate with dimples named Cory. "And taking this ship from girls will be like taking candy from babies!"

"I am First Mate EJ Payne of the Merriweather," *EJ says, stepping up on a wooden crate to appear a little taller. "And like it or not, girls can do anything that boys can do."*

"Arrrgh, now there's where you're wrong, me beauty." Weird Beard was talking for himself this time. "Girls can't get to ramming speed like boys can. Full speed ahead!"

The pirate ship lurches forward, straight toward the Merriweather. *In a split-second decision, EJ yanks the helm and swings her ship at the pirate ship.*

BOOM! The two boats careen into each other, rattling the bones of everybody on board.

"Good form!" Weird Beard laughs. "Again!"

"Is that all you've got?" EJ shouts. "It felt like your ship just bounced right off the Merriweather!"

The ships pass each other and circle around, readying for another collision.

"EJ, I found these under the seats!" Katy showed EJ two double-barreled water guns.

"Excellent!" EJ smiled at Katy and grabbed one, keeping it low enough in the boat that Isaac and Cory couldn't see it. "Full water assault when I say 'now.' "

"Got it!" Katy grinned.

EJ held the gun between her knees and grasped the steering wheel with both hands as she squared up to the boys' boat.

Just before EJ was about to jam the boat's throttle to the floor for ramming speed, she heard a pop of static come from the floating boat dock behind them.

"ATTENTION: girls in the red bumper boat!" Gene's voice seemed to be amplified over the surface of the lake. "The day camper's lifejacket isn't secured properly. You must snap the top buckle *now*, or I will take away your boating privileges."

EJ saw that Katy's top buckle had gotten unclipped somehow, so she reached over and snapped it together quickly.

"There, we got it." EJ waved and gave the thumbs-up sign at Gene. "We're good!"

First Mate EJ urges the Merriweather *ahead at full speed, eyeing the oncoming pirate ship. If she doesn't time this right, it could be a head-on crash that might sink both ships.*

"Cannons ready," EJ gives the order to Katy.

"Ready," Katy replies.

"Steady. . ." EJ waits for the right moment. "NOW!"

EJ and Katy raised their water guns and sent two colossal streams of water toward the boys. EJ's hit Cory right in the chest, and Katy's cascaded like a waterfall on the top of Isaac's head. EJ wished she could've taken a picture of their shocked faces.

Isaac lost control of the steering wheel as he wiped water out of his eyes, but their boat still sped ahead.

"Ahhh!" Cory tried to grab the wheel, but it was too late. "Look out!"

The boys' bumper boat did a spectacular spin and smacked into the floating boat dock—hard—before bouncing off, no harm done to the boat or the boys. The dock lurched from the impact, throwing Gene off balance so he stutter-stepped off the side of the dock, headfirst into the water.

A couple seconds later, Gene broke the surface of the water, coughing up lake water and arms and legs flailing before he got his feet under him in the shoulder-deep water. With his red hair hanging in strings on his face and water dripping off him, he looked a little more like a drowned fox rather than a camp counselor. He slowly lifted the megaphone from the water, the strap still firmly around his wrist.

The campers in the boats and on the shore collectively held their breath, wondering what would come next.

He pulled the trigger, and the megaphone siren gave the saddest little wail EJ had ever heard before the sound faded and sputtered to silence.

A cheer erupted from the crowd. Isaac didn't know it then, but it would be a Camp Christian story that would be told for years to come.

Chapter 12

OUTWIT. OUTPLAY. OUT IN THE WILDERNESS

Dear Diary,

It's Thursday, the day campers are back at home, and
this afternoon we're heading out into the woods to sleep
in tents tonight in the wilderness. I don't really know
what to expect because most of my
camping has been in Nana and Pops's
Winnebago. I guess we do stay in tents
at family camp—but Dad lets us watch movies on his
laptop at night. I don't think anyone would call that kind
of camping "roughing it."

I kind of hope wilderness camp will be something like
that TV show called *Survivor*. It's one of Dad's favorite
shows, and sometimes I watch it with him. The best
thing about *Survivor* is the
immunity challenges that the
contestants play. My least favorite
thing about it is the bugs. And the
nasty food they have to eat to stay alive. (Dad told me
about one time when the contestants cooked a rat and ate
it! GROSS!)

Macy told me she's a little nervous about being out in the woods in the dark. I told her there's nothing to worry about, and I'll protect her. Unless there are baby alligators in the woods, in which case I'll be terrified, too. But if there are fuzzy bunnies, we'll be fine. (Honestly, Diary, I had no idea I was such a wimp!)

So I'm packing my backpack for overnight in the woods. (Note to self: don't forget to pack the bug spray!) You're going with me, Diary. So at least if I don't survive out there, there will be a record of who I was.

EJ

EJ slapped her left elbow, ending the life of one of about a million mosquitoes in the woods.

"Yuck!" she said, wiping away the remnants of the bloodthirsty bug with her T-shirt sleeve.

The girls of dorm E were making the mile-long hike to wilderness camp. Each girl toted a backpack and a sleeping bag and pillow under each arm. Susan led the way, stopping the group every now and then to point out an interesting tree or bird.

"Everybody here?" Susan asked, doing a quick head count. "CoraLee, you still with us, girl?"

"I'm here!" CoraLee sounded breathless due to the fact that her backpack was positively stuffed with enough pink ruffles and accessories for a weeklong stay in the wilderness. Back at the dorm, EJ overheard CoraLee telling Susan that Michael Draper "volunteered" to carry her camp gear out to the campsite, but Susan said no, CoraLee had to carry her own stuff because boys were absolutely forbidden to set foot on the girls' campsite. EJ thought for sure CoraLee would pack a little lighter after that, but apparently fashion was more important than being practical.

"For some of you, this might be your first time camping out in the woods, so I want to show you something to avoid," Susan said.

Susan gathered the girls around a tree that had poison ivy growing up the trunk and pointed out the way the plant was divided into three leaflets. "That's how you can identify poison ivy," the counselor explained. "Remember the old saying, 'Leaves of three, let it be.' "

They passed a pretty little brook and a sign that pointed in opposite directions, one to the girls' latrine and one to the boys' latrine.

"Susan, what's a latrine?" Anna Baker asked the question that everyone else was wondering.

"The outdoor commode," Susan said matter-of-factly. Some of the girls still looked confused, so she made it even clearer by saying, "The outdoor toilet."

"The outdoor WHAT?" CoraLee's voice reached a shrill pitch at the end of the question.

"It's not all that bad," Susan said, trying to hide a chuckle. "Besides, this is *wilderness* camp, ladies. No plumbing, no electricity. Let's enjoy God's creation to its fullest!"

EJ grinned at Susan. She thought the camp counselor might just be the best adult she knew. She made another mental note to ask Susan what she needed to do to become a camp counselor someday.

A few minutes later, the trail opened up to a large clearing marked by a carved wooden sign that said GIRLS DORM E. Ten small tents were set up in a circle, and in the middle was a fire pit surrounded by several large stumps that looked like the perfect place to sit to enjoy the fire.

"Home sweet home, ladies!" Susan said, smiling. "Pair up and find a tent."

There was a moment of scurrying as everyone found a partner and sprinted for a tent. EJ and Macy grabbed hands and ran to the opposite side of the tent circle to claim their space.

Inside the tent they found two thin air mattresses lying parallel on the floor. The tent was just big enough for them to crawl inside, unroll their sleeping bags on the mattresses, plop their pillows at the head, and set their backpacks on the floor between their sleeping areas.

EJ and Macy sat cross-legged on their sleeping bags and gulped water from plastic bottles to try to cool down from their hike.

EJ pulls the bottle away from her mouth and gasps.

"Macy, slow down!" she says frantically. "We never know how long it'll be until we find fresh drinking water again."

"You're right, EJ," Macy says solemnly, twisting the cap on her water bottle and stowing it in her bag. "What's for supper tonight? Do we have any rice left, or are we going to have to scout for edible bugs?"

"The rest of the tribe ate all the rice this morning," EJ says. "Looks like it's bugs for us tonight. And maybe a mango or two if we can find them."

The best friends are braving the wilderness together with the hopes of being the last two standing—to win Survivor *and the cash prize that goes along with it. It's a battle of wits and survival skills, and one they are both committed to.*

"Girls, come out of your tents as soon as you have your beds made," Susan called. "We're going to have a little competition against the other dorms."

EJ and Macy gathered with the other girls near Susan's tent. Susan crawled out of her tent a few moments later, a red bandanna folded and tied around her head like a headband and a bundle of red fabric under her arm.

"Here are our team bandannas," Susan said, passing out red handkerchiefs. "You can wear them however you'd like; they just have to be visible."

Girls got creative with their bandannas, some loosely tying theirs around their necks like a cowboy, others wearing them as armbands or bracelets. One girl tied it in a knot around her leg, just above her knee.

"Are we ready to win?" Susan, the leader of the all-female tribe, asks.

"Yeah!" the girls shout back.

"Then follow me," she says, leading them deeper into the woods.

EJ tightens the red bandanna around her head, keeping her hair away from her face. She's feeling lucky to be on the red tribe since red's her favorite color and is, in her opinion, the most powerful-looking color.

Susan leads the red tribe to a clearing, and they come face-to-face with the four other tribes—yellow, purple, blue, and green. As the crowd parts, the red tribe gets its first glance at an epic-looking obstacle course that crosses over a creek flowing through the clearing.

"Whoa."

As EJ took in the sights of the obstacle course, she realized she didn't really need to imagine anything—what was going on in front of her was just as good (if not better) than she could've made up in her head.

Susan explained each part: a climbing cargo net led to a platform about ten feet off the ground. Once the entire tribe got on the platform, they had to complete a wooden puzzle that unlocked a hatch to a slide off of the platform, back to the ground. Next was a maze made out of hay bales stacked five feet high—with only one correct way through, Susan said—and lots of dead ends.

For the final part of the obstacle course, Susan pointed to a rope bridge about forty feet long that spanned the fast-moving creek. EJ didn't think "rope bridge" was a very good description of what she saw. It was more like three thick ropes suspended across the creek: one to walk on and two that were waist high to hold on to and keep your balance.

"The first team to get everyone across the creek wins," Susan said. "And the winning team will take back to their campsite the fixin's for a hot dog and s'mores roast."

"What do the losers eat for dinner?" someone shouted from the orange team.

"Something we like to call a 'wilderness buffet,' " Susan said, smiling. "Beef jerky and trail mix."

The crowd of girls let out a groan. After finding out there were hot dogs and s'mores on the line, the wilderness buffet sounded downright disappointing.

"Okay, girls, here we go!" Susan cupped her hands around her mouth—nearly as effective as Gene's megaphone, but much less annoying. "On your marks. Get set. GO!"

EJ's quick reflexes helped her sprint out ahead of the other girls, and she was the first from the red team to jump onto the cargo net, climbing as fast as she could. She glanced back to see the hungry eyes of her teammates. Hungry for the win—and hungry for the hot dogs and s'mores.

EJ lost her foothold on the cargo net, and she dangled for a second, dangerously close to losing her hand grips and falling on top of her teammates at her heels.

"Keep going, EJ!" Susan cheered from below the cargo net. "You've got this, red team!"

EJ regained her footing and looked up to see she was only a couple of feet from the top of the platform. Suddenly Macy leaned over the edge and smiled down at EJ, offering a hand to help her up the last little bit.

"That's my best friend—the gymnast!" EJ called to no one. "Thanks, Mace!"

EJ and Macy sat on the edge of red team's platform and helped their teammates up. CoraLee was having an especially difficult time with the cargo net because she was wearing high-heeled sandals instead of athletic shoes like everyone else.

"CoraLee, just kick off your shoes!" Susan yelled. "It'll make it easier for you to get up the net—I promise!"

"I'm *not* kicking these off just to get lost in the underbrush!" CoraLee clung desperately to the cargo net, unable to go up or down. "They're *designer!*"

"And they're super cute, but they aren't going to help the team win," Susan said. "Toss them down to me, and I'll keep them safe."

CoraLee poked her arms through the cargo net, reached down to her feet, and retrieved the impractical shoes before dropping them into Susan's outstretched hands below.

"Got 'em—now go!" Susan motioned to CoraLee to hurry.

EJ had never really thought CoraLee was very athletic, so she was surprised at how quickly the barefooted CoraLee scrambled up the cargo net and was catching her breath on the edge of the platform next to Macy.

"Who is good at puzzles?" Sara Powers asked.

"Me!" EJ and CoraLee said in unison.

"Okay, both of you, over here," Sara said, pointing at the wooden puzzle pieces.

EJ and CoraLee narrowed their eyes at each other. Could they really work together?

"Two heads *are* better than one," EJ said, testing the waters with CoraLee.

"No way am I eating beef jerky," CoraLee said. "Let's do this thing!"

EJ and CoraLee spread out the puzzle pieces on the platform, and the rest of the team formed a half circle around them, cheering them on. They would have to assemble the puzzle in a frame that was built into the hatch that led to the slide, and only when the puzzle was completed would the hatch swing open.

"I see letters and a design," CoraLee said as she finished flipping over the puzzle pieces to all face the same way.

"It seems familiar. . . ." EJ closed her eyes for a moment and a picture started to take shape. "C. H. R. I. . . . It's the Camp Christian logo!" she shouted, opening her eyes.

"Yes! You're right!" CoraLee picked up the first four letters—CAMP—and put them in the puzzle frame. "Nice job, EJ!"

EJ and CoraLee finished the puzzle in no time flat, and soon everyone was barreling down the slide to the beginning of the maze. EJ was running on pure adrenaline now. The race against the other teams was extremely close.

The red team entered their maze and immediately hit a dead end. The narrow passageway and tall hay bale walls made for difficult communication among the girls, so there was a lot of confusion about which way to go and who was leading. EJ was getting frustrated quickly. She jumped up into the air to try to see which way they should go. All of a sudden, she realized there was someone on her team that could see above the walls without jumping.

"Sara, *you* have to lead us through the maze!" EJ said. "Guys, let Sara Powers go to the front of the line!"

"What? Why me?" Sara looked confused.

"You're tall! You can see over the walls so you know which way to go!" EJ said, nudging her forward. "Hurry!"

Sara got to the front of the line and quickly led the girls through the maze, only hitting one more dead-end that was in a really tricky spot, so no one blamed her.

The red team was the first out of the maze, and they all ran toward the rope bridge, nearly tripping over each other as several girls unsteadily made their way out on the rope. A few seconds later, five of them screamed and fell in the creek, wet from the waist down.

"Hold on, everyone, we have to make a plan!" EJ shouted. "Anybody have an idea?"

"I do!" Macy held up her hand.

"Okay, go," EJ said.

"It's like when I'm training for gymnastics—you have to leave enough room between you and the next person, or you'll mess each other up," Macy said. "So the first person should go, and then the next person should wait until the first person is halfway across. That way you won't feel the person next to you moving the rope as much as you would if you were right next to each other."

"Yeah, that's how we ended up in the creek," said Alexa, one of wet-from-the-waist-down girls. "That sounds like a good plan!"

"It'll take patience, though," Macy warned. "The other teams are catching up with us, and we're going to want to go faster and send more than one person across at once, but slow and steady is going to win it for us."

Macy coached the team across, one by one, and her plan worked really well. The other teams quickly finished the maze and tried the all-at-once approach, but no team got more than one or two girls across that way before they ended up in the creek. By that time, the red team had a nice lead, but the blue team was copying their one-at-a-time approach and was quickly catching up.

"We need to pick up the pace, so just try to go a *little* faster," Macy said, glancing over her shoulder at the blue team. EJ was on the rope now, and she concentrated on keeping her center of balance directly over her feet. She gripped the hand ropes loosely so she could slide her hands along them without getting rope burn. Soon she stepped off the rope bridge on the other side and immediately started cheering on the remaining teammates behind her.

EJ saw the blue team only had three people left on the far creek bank, but there were four left on the red team's bank. Both teams were shouting encouragement to their teammates, but the blue team was nearing a fever pitch—it was like they could already taste the gooey s'more deliciousness.

The last member of the blue team started on the rope bridge at the same time CoraLee started for the red team—that still left Macy on the far bank. Apparently being barefoot was a real asset to walking across a rope, because CoraLee walked across the rope so fast that she almost caught up with the girl in front of her.

EJ saw Macy's eyes light up as she watched CoraLee's quick trip across the rope. In a flash, Macy removed her shoes and socks and eased out onto the rope. EJ heard the roar of the blue team and saw that their final teammate was more than halfway across the rope bridge already. It seemed like there was no way the red team would be able to pull out a win, but EJ knew better than to count out Macy Russell. With a clear path in front of her, Macy took a deep breath and pranced gracefully across the rope, her hands stretched out at her sides to keep her balance. Part gymnastic feat, part lovely dance, she looked perfectly at ease coming across the rope in her bare feet, pointed toes and all. The red team seemed to hold its breath as she floated toward them, passing the girl on the blue team, who was struggling to keep her balance. At the end of the bridge, Macy vaulted off the suspended rope and did a front handspring onto the ground. The red team went crazy. EJ could already taste the fire-roasted hot dog—with relish and extra ketchup!

"Flashlights off in two minutes, girls!" Susan called from her tent.

EJ zipped the tent door shut and shined her flashlight beam at Macy, who was already snug in her sleeping bag.

"Hey, my eyes! You're blinding me, EJ!" Macy said, pulling the edge of her sleeping bag over her head to block the light.

"Oops, sorry." EJ flashed the light in her own eyes and grinned. "There. Now we're even." Now blind as well, EJ groped toward her sleeping bag and crawled inside.

"All I can see right now are those green blobs you get when someone takes a picture with a flash," Macy said, laughing and grabbing at the nonexistent blobs in front of her eyes.

"Oooh, yeah, those are so weird!" EJ laughed. "Want some gummy worms? I still have a whole bag left from Aunt CJ's care package."

Macy looked conflicted. "But I already brushed my teeth."

EJ grinned, pulled the package of gummy worms from her backpack, and ripped it open. "So did I, but I won't tell anybody if you won't."

"All right," Macy said. "But just this once." Macy took three gummy worms from the bag and started gnawing on one.

"Lights off, ladies!" Susan called. "Good night!"

"Good night, Susan!" EJ and Macy joined in with the chorus of girls.

EJ turned off her flashlight and watched the orange light from the dying campfire dance on the wall of the tent as she chewed on a lemon-flavored gummy worm.

The girls were both quiet for a minute; the only sounds were an occasional giggle from a nearby tent and the constant chirp of crickets in the woods. EJ's brain started thinking about what she absolutely *didn't* want to think about.

"Hey, Mace?" EJ whispered.

"Yeah?"

EJ took a deep breath before she started a very long sentence. "I haven't told you something because I knew you were worried about moving away and I was worried, too, but now that you're not moving away, I think I should tell you that my parents have been acting strange this summer in the same way your parents were acting strange, and I think it's because *we're* moving away."

"Are you sure?" Macy asked.

"Pretty sure," EJ said. "I'm an excellent detective. And all the clues point to it."

Macy held out the gummy worm bag to EJ, who grabbed two more and shoved them in her mouth, hoping they would help the nervous churning of her stomach as she shared her secret with her best friend.

"You know what really stinks?" EJ asked, lying back on her sleeping bag and staring at the stars through the mesh window at the top of their tent. "We're just kids. There's nothing we can do about. . .anything! Adults make all the decisions, do what they want, and even keep secrets from us. It makes me feel so. . .so. . ."

"Helpless?" Macy finished EJ's thought.

"Exactly," EJ said, sighing.

"I don't want to move away," EJ said quietly. "If a miracle

happens and we don't move, I'll never say a bad thing about Spooner again."

"Don't make a promise you can't keep, EJ." There was a hint of a smile in Macy's voice. "It *is* a boring town."

"Okay, I'll *try* to say more good things than bad things about Spooner." EJ grinned. "Is that better?"

"That seems more believable," Macy said, yawning. "And anyway, one miracle has already happened. We're not moving. So I think a miracle can happen for you, too."

"Maybe you're right," EJ said, unconvinced. "Good night, Mace."

"Good night, EJ."

Chapter 13

WONDER GIRL

Dear Diary,

Last night after lights out, we had a furry visitor to our campsite. And by "furry visitor" I mean a bear. And by a "bear" I mean the dorm mom from dorm A dressed up in a goofy bear costume she borrowed from the camp cooks. Apparently they thought it'd be fun to prank us since we were the only dorm to eat actual food for supper—and boy, were those hot dogs and s'mores amazing!

I guess dorm A's plan was to make us think our leftover food attracted a grizzly to our campsite. Except Susan (aka, the best dorm mom ever) heard them giggling as they came through the woods, so she quickly woke us all up and we were ready for them.

When the "bear" and group of girls stepped foot in our tent circle, we all jumped out from behind our tents and pelted them with our leftover marshmallows. You should've seen the looks on their faces, Diary! Several girls

screamed and ran into the woods, but soon we were
all laughing. We even shared our leftover
chocolate with them, and then the dorm
moms let us play a game of sardines in the
woods before we all had to go back to bed.

    Last night was fun, but I think today will
be even better. It's our day for the high ropes course!
EJ

EJ wondered if it was just her imagination or if the wooden tower she was sitting on—thirty feet off the ground—actually swayed a little bit. It didn't help that the sound of the gentle summer breeze seemed extra loud in the helmet strapped on her head.

EJ, Macy, and the rest of the girls from dorm E sat on the large platform, each girl strapped into a harness fit around her legs and waist. Susan had already talked them through safety procedures for the high ropes, and they had just broken into pairs and were assigned to a counselor. EJ felt like the luckiest girl in the world because she and Macy were with Susan.

"Okay, girls, ready to climb to the tall tower?" Susan pointed to the zip line tower about forty feet above them.

"Let's do it!" Macy slapped palms with Susan in a high five.

"I think I can, I think I can," EJ chanted under her breath.

"EJ, I don't understand why you're nervous," Macy said. "You spent hours and hours up in a harness like this during the nativity play last Christmas when you were the angel. This doesn't seem that much different to me."

"Well, first of all, I was only like ten feet off the ground," EJ said. "And second of all, Dad had the other end of the rope, and I knew he wasn't going to let me fall."

"So you trust your dad more than you trust the safety harness," Susan said. "Right on—I totally get that. But do you trust *me* enough to at least climb up to the zip line tower with us?"

EJ gulped and nodded. No way was she going to disappoint Susan.

The counselor checked their safety equipment, and then the trio began to climb the ladder—Macy in the lead followed by EJ, and Susan bringing up the rear.

"Do you girls want to know a secret about me?" Susan asked as they climbed.

"Ooo, yeah! I love secrets." EJ glanced back at Susan but snapped her head forward again quickly when she realized how high up they actually were.

"I'm afraid of heights." Susan laughed.

"Good one." EJ reached the top of the ladder and stepped onto the zip line platform. "Now it's my turn to tell a joke. Knock-knock."

"No, really, I'm actually afraid of heights," Susan said as she hopped onto the platform, obviously at ease even seventy feet off the ground. "Getting my high-ropes certification was almost impossible for me because of it."

EJ mentally scratched camp counselor off her career list.

"Then why did you do it?" EJ asked, clutching her safety line so tightly that her knuckles turned white.

"I've wanted to be a counselor at Camp Christian since I was your age, and I had to get my certification to do it," Susan said, turning toward the girls. "So I worked with my instructor on the ground until I trusted the safety equipment. Then I knew that even if I fell off the very highest platform, the safety equipment would protect me. So really, I don't have anything to be afraid of."

EJ didn't look so sure. "Susan, how much weight can these safety lines actually hold?" she asked, eyeballing the rope she was clinging to.

"Waaaay more than what you weigh, EJ girl," Susan said. "Watch." Without warning, she bent her knees slightly, leaned back, and fell off the platform. EJ and Macy gasped as they saw her free fall, but in the blink of an eye, the safety cable caught her so she was dangling only about two feet lower than before.

"See?" Susan grinned as she pulled herself onto the platform with ease. "We're completely safe."

EJ loosened her grip on the cable, a little less terrified—even peeking over the edge of the platform.

"There are lots of things you can choose to put your trust in," Susan said as she unhooked the zip line equipment from the cable above. "But I've learned that if I put my life in something I know I can trust, I don't have to be nervous when something crazy or scary happens."

Like moving away, EJ thought.

"So, EJ—you're going first and showing Macy how it's done!" Susan said.

"I—I am?" EJ stammered.

"Yeah, come on, EJ—I know you can do it." Macy gave her a reassuring smile.

Susan had EJ lie facedown on top of the zip line sling, and she attached EJ's safety harness. Then Susan wrapped it around EJ's torso and legs, leaving her arms free. Finally, Susan flipped a switch that lifted EJ about three feet off the platform. The harness hugged her snugly, like she was a human burrito.

Looking down on the top of the platform, EJ saw there were words carved into the wooden planks underneath her.

"Hey, what's that?" EJ pointed to the words.

"Read them out loud," Susan said.

" 'This is my command—be strong and courageous!' " EJ read. " 'Do not be afraid or discouraged. For the Lord your God is with you wherever you go.' Joshua 1:9."

"No matter what's going on—whether I'm flying high on the

zip line or if my feet are on the ground—*that's* what I choose to put my trust in," Susan said. "*Who* I put my trust in."

"Okay, I'm ready," EJ said. "Let's do it."

EJ closed her eyes as Susan counted off: "Three, two, one—fly!" As soon as Susan let go, EJ felt her full body weight tug on the zip line sling, hugging her a little tighter in an oddly comforting way. Gravity kicked in, and she heard the *zizzz* of the zip line above her, slowly at first. A gust of warm summer wind blew her hair off her face as she prayed, "I trust You, God. Starting now, no matter what happens—even if we have to move to Antarctica—I trust You."

EJ opened her eyes just as she soared off the edge of the platform, gaining speed by the second. The beauty of the clear sky above her and the green valley below made her chest swell with excitement as a laugh exploded from her throat. *I wonder if this is what people mean when they say I have my head in the clouds,* she thought.

EJ stretched her arms straight out in front of her. . . .

Wonder Girl zooms over the top of the city buildings, making a game of dodging the skyscrapers and flying as low as she can over the shorter buildings. She uses her super eyesight to scan the ground for trouble—a kitten in a tree, a lost child, a bad guy scheming to take over the world—but all seems well, so she settles in to her flying pattern, enjoying the view. With her cape flapping behind her, Wonder Girl glances to her right and sees her loyal sidekick, Bert the Power Pooch, flying a few feet away. She gives him a thumbs-up, and he wags his tail and barks a happy yip before twisting into three perfectly executed barrel rolls. She laughs as Bert flies off to scatter a flock of geese. The only thing he loves more than crime fighting is messing up their V formation. In the distance, EJ hears excited shouting of her adoring public.

"Wooooo-hooooo!" Susan cupped her hands around her mouth and shouted. "Get it, girl!"

"Yeah, EJ!" Macy yelled. "Looking good!"

EJ sat in the grass on the hillside overlooking the lake, her legs stretched out in front of her with Dad's Bible and a pen on her lap. She took in a deep breath, puffed out her chest, and held in the fresh camp air a moment before exhaling. The lake water looked so smooth and perfect in the late-afternoon sun—just like a mirror that reflected the billowy cotton-ballish clouds in the sky. A second later, the glass shattered when a fish jumped near the shore and sent a thousand ripples out in all directions—circles within circles. A dragonfly the size of a large paperclip landed on the toe of her left Converse All-Star, the insect's green and blue body glistening like a jewel in the sun.

This might be my favorite spot in the entire universe, EJ thought.

She gently shooed away the dragonfly, sat cross-legged, and opened the Bible across her knees. She flipped through a few of the thin pages before she came to one of Dad's handwritten notes in the margin in the Old Testament book Jeremiah. First she read the highlighted Bible text. " 'For I know the plans I have for you,' declares the Lord, 'plans to prosper you and not to harm you, plans to give you hope and a future.' "

Then she squinted to read the note, written in Dad's recognizable handwriting:

God's plans > David Payne's plans

She smiled and ran her index finger over the writing, imagining Dad as a camper, maybe sitting in this exact spot by the lake when he wrote these words in his brand-new Bible. She uncapped her pen and wrote underneath Dad's note:

God's plans > EJ Payne's worries

The dinner bell rang. EJ capped the pen and stuck it in her pocket. Then she shut the Bible and tucked the special book in the crook of her arm before skipping up the hill toward the dining hall. What was that she smelled? Garlic! Spaghetti and meatballs, maybe!

"Attention, girl in the Converse sneakers—!" EJ jumped and whirled around to see Gene, speaking a little too loudly as he stood behind her in line for supper. Apparently without his megaphone, he thought he had to shout to be heard. "You're EJ Payne, right?"

"That's me," she said.

Gene thrust an envelope toward her. "This came for you in yesterday's mail. I'm sorry you didn't get it then, but it was caught in the front flap of the mail bag, and I didn't see it till now."

EJ took the letter and recognized Mom's handwriting.

"What'd you get?" Macy asked as EJ tore open the envelope.

"It's a letter from Mom," she said, smiling. "I was starting to think she forgot about me!"

To my darlingest, sweetest, most belovedest EJ in the entire history of EJs,

177

Did the opening greeting of this note make you throw up a little bit? I bet it did. But even though I wrote it that way to make you smile, it's still true, and I love you very much.

Your dad and I were going to wait until you got home from camp, but we decided that we couldn't wait any longer, so I'm sending you this letter with some BIG NEWS.

Uh-oh, here we go, thought EJ. *God, are You still here? I need You to be with me right now. . .these are Your plans—not mine.*

I'm talking the biggest, most exciting news for the Payne family in such a long time. News that is so big that your aunt CJ could write an entire front-page newspaper article about it. Gigantic. Colossal. Enormous. Huge. Are you ready to find out what it is?

Spit it out, Mom! EJ thought.

Well, you'll just have to wait a little while longer.

I know this summer has been difficult for you, EJ. I've seen you get frustrated when Dad and I left for mysterious meetings, and I think you probably noticed that I've been more emotional than normal. Even when you were brave enough to ask questions, we didn't give you straight answers because we didn't want to get your hopes up, and the truth of the matter is that we couldn't share confidential information with you until we met with the lawyers to get everything sorted out.

Lawyers? You're killing me, Mom.

Here it is: You're going to have a new sister.

"You're PREGNANT?" EJ yelled in excited surprise at the paper in her hand.

"Wha–?" Macy's question got cut off by EJ, who held up a finger in a "wait just a minute" motion. She had to read on to see what else Mom had written.

No, I'm not pregnant.

For the past several months, your dad and I have been praying, asking God to show us His plans for our family. And soon we both felt like God was asking us to consider something—something that actually scared us a little bit. And I'm ashamed to say it, but we ignored what God was telling us. We just put it in the back of our minds, thinking maybe God would forget about it.

Then an opportunity came through our church at the beginning of the summer that was just like God shouting, "Hey, Paynes, this is what I want you to do. I've worked out the details, so all you have to do is say yes! Will you trust Me?" You see, there was a young woman who had given birth to a baby girl, but because of her situation, she couldn't give her daughter a very good life. And God brought this baby to us so that she can learn and grow in His love—and ours, too.

This is a big deal for the whole family, EJ. And although we know at this point that the new little Payne is cleared to come live with us soon, we all have to be on board with the plan. It's my hope and prayer that you'll say yes—that we'll welcome this baby into our family together.

I can't wait to see you and hear all of your amazing camp stories when we pick you up on Saturday morning. I've missed you so much this week!

Love,
Mom

EJ folded the letter, held it in her hands, and stared at it, furrowing her brow in concentration. She mentally went through the list of clues:

1. Mom crying. EJ thought back to the scene she saw before her. It was normal for the family to pray together, but the crying was new. Maybe, just maybe, Mom and Nana weren't crying because they were sad. Maybe they were— happy? EJ didn't understand why someone would cry when they were happy, but adults *were* strange like that.

2. Dad leaving to meet with the board "stuff. . .about the thing." Mom's letter said that the adoption came about because of their connection with Vine Street Community Church, so obviously the board would have to be part of that discussion.

3. Mom and Dad leaving before family game night. Meetings with lawyers. Of course! That had to be it.

Not only was EJ *not* moving, but she was getting a new *sister*!

EJ picks up the toddler wearing the tiny red Converse All-Stars.

The little girl's chubby hands reach out to squeeze EJ's face from both sides, making her cheeks bulge like a chipmunk. EJ grins and crosses her eyes at her little sister. The toddler squeals and giggles.

"Um, EJ?" Macy asked cautiously.

"What? Oh Macy—sorry." EJ's daydream faded into the background.

"Is everything okay?" Macy asked.

"You know what?" EJ said. "Everything is crazy and weird and surprising. But it doesn't feel scary anymore. I have a lot to tell you!"

July 26

Dear Diary,

Saturday morning of camp couldn't have been more different than Monday morning. Remember how my entire dorm woke up even before the wake-up bell on Monday? Well, this morning every single girl in the bunks would've slept WAY past the bell. . .if Susan had let us. Instead, she woke us up with the most terribly annoying camp song I've ever heard. It started out as a cute melody about little birds sleeping in a nest, and

then the song took an awful turn when Susan yelled "QUIET!" and "GOOD MORNING, GOOD MORNING!" at

the end of the song. Susan laughed and said it was a camp tradition.

I said I thought it was one tradition that should die.

Mom, Dad, and Isaac picked me up from camp after breakfast, and even though I love camp, I was happy to be going home. So I said good-bye to Susan, Gene, the cooks (dressed in normal clothes—Camp Christian T-shirts and shorts—for the first time all week), and everyone else

I met at camp, and we piled into the minivan with my stuff. Isaac talked the entire forty-minute drive home about day camp and how much fun he had and about our epic bumper boat battle and how funny it was that Gene fell in the lake and how he got so many high fives from the older campers after he waterlogged Gene's megaphone and even though he didn't mean to do it, it was a pretty awesome accident. (You get the idea—the kid is a motormouth. Luckily for Isaac, I was so tired I just let him talk.)

When we got home, there was a giant pile of bags and boxes on the front porch—donations from people at church to help us prepare for the arrival for the new little Payne that will be joining our family sometime in the next few days. Crib and car seat and high chair and diapers and wipes and rash cream (gross) and clothes and blankets and bottles and teething rings and on and on! Who would've guessed a baby required so much junk? I picked up something that looked like an eye dropper with a rubber ball on the end and asked Mom what it was. She said it was something

called a "nasal aspirator," and that it was one of the best
baby inventions ever. Then she got distracted
when Mrs. McCallister stopped by to drop
off a bag full of frilly pink baby dresses (no
way am I letting a sister of mine wear those
things!), so I didn't get a chance to ask her what a nasal
aspirator does. I guess I'll find out sooner or later.

This baby adoption is going to mean big changes for
us, and honestly, I don't know what to expect. But
she's a girl, so I would think that she's not as gross
or annoying as Isaac was as a baby (right?). But
even though I don't know what's going to happen,
one thing I learned at camp is that God does know—and
He can handle it, no matter what "it" is.

Dad is calling up the stairs for me to come down.
We're having pizza for supper and playing games in the
tree house, but first we're going to hang our old baby swing
that we didn't throw out after the Swing Set Switcharoo.
(A clue to the mystery I obviously overlooked. I guess I still
have a thing or two to learn about detective work!)

So it's on to another adventure for the Payne family—

this one starring EJ as big sister extraordinaire!

EJ

P.S. Oh, I guess I haven't told you the baby's name yet. After everything that's happened this summer, it seems oddly appropriate. The baby's name is Faith. Faith Nicole Payne.

About the Author

Annie Tipton made up her first story at the ripe old age of two when she asked her mom to write it down for her. (Hey, she was just two—she didn't know how to make letters yet!) Since then she has read and written many words as a student, newspaper reporter, author, and editor. Annie loves snow (which is a good thing because she lives in Ohio), wearing scarves, sushi, Scrabble, and spending time with friends and family.

What readers are saying about Diary of a Real Payne

"Parents that love each other, a family that laughs and has fun together, friends that take care of each other. . . what more could you ask for in a story?"
-Michele P., *Faith, Family, and Fridays* blog

"Not only does Annie Tipton present the story in a fun way (lots of giggles!), but it really is a wonderful story of compassion and God's love."
-Rebekah T., *There Will Be a $5 Charge for Whining* blog

"This book is simply fabulous."
-Crystal H., *Crystal Starr* blog

"[It's] one of those books that grabs your attention the very moment you pick it up. . . . My children didn't want me to stop reading."
-Candy F., *Strategic Shopping* blog